WHEN PARIS WAS HER LOVER

A Novel

HEIDI M. HARRISON

EMERALD HOUSE PUBLISHING

www.emeraldhpublishing.com

Printed in the United States of America
First edition: July 2022

Cover art by Clare Colins
Book and cover design by Kathy Campbell of Gorham Printing
Photograph in Paris courtesy of Brune d'Esna

To my beautiful ninety-two-year-old mother

who, every day, reminds me how survival

and love are intricately woven together.

"What tree is there that the wind has not shaken?"

PASHTO PROVERB

Prologue

PARIS, 2000

Marlene Robinson stood under the Eiffel Tower, alone. She let the delicate latticework engulf her, charm her as it soared into the air. In that moment there were no boundaries, no limits as her mind wandered to fifteen years earlier when, for her much younger self, Paris had been her lover. Everywhere she walked this day so many years later, she felt seduced. The city reached all her senses and filled her with the sublime.

Paris never wanted Marlene to forget her, although Marlene had during her absence. Today she experienced a towering agelessness, and she remembered someone once telling her that a lover once is a lover forever. Once one has been embraced by another who has rested and sunk into *les profondeurs* of one's existence, their imprint never fades.

In her promenade that morning, she became intoxicated by fragrances; a desirous mixture flitted through her nostrils. The smells of rising yeast mixed with butter and vanilla, cinnamon and chocolate oozed out of quiet neighborhoods where bakers pulled pans out of ovens. On another street in another kitchen, potatoes sizzled in olive oil and *herbes de provence*. The sounds of Paris filled her ears as well. The wind wafted over the Seine. The morning traffic roared around the city. The resonance of a cello and a violin in a church transformed the timbre of her soul. Marlene's insatiability overtook her, the lifetime of cravings she had never actualized.

She looked up at *La tour Eiffel*, feeling its gross wisps of metal envelop her like a scarf, gently wrapped around her neck, silk folded into the gracefulness of her arms, grazing her contours. *I have grown; no longer am I a child, as was the case when first we paired. I was behind a closed door then, sealed in my chambers. Now, fifteen years later, I am ready for her.* She sank deeply into *le paysage* of her being as the breeze whispered through the openings of the Tower. Somewhere deeply embedded in her consciousness was a voice, a whisper, a quiet murmur: *Let every part of you,* it said, *meet the rain on the pavement, where the Louvre joins* les colonnades, *timelessness bathed in history. We are ancient, all of us,* the whispering continued, as boats floated up and down the Seine. *There are tastes to savor, notes to serenade your soul on a Sunday morning, when leaves fly every- where, fluttering around your eyelashes, and landing gently at your feet.*

PART ONE

Les Rencontres

CHAPTER ONE

San Francisco

1985

Marlene lived on Haight Street at Divisadero, where the Muni buses sped through the streets, and often, late at night, women would scream, curse a lover, and open a window and throw his belongings down onto the pavement. It was the tail end of free speech and free love that had spilled out onto Haight-Ashbury. AIDS had taken its place, and where once there was a happy blend of stoned hipsters filling the parks and sidewalks, now there was an eerie glow, a somber end to a rolled-out party. Every day after her work as a teacher at a local childcare center, Marlene would throw her bag on the floor of her apartment, put on her tennis shoes, and walk. She often ambled down Haight Street and would end up at a café or at Golden Gate Park. She loved the hills of the Castro, the old houses, the glorified *grandes dames* of this beloved city she called home. Not wanting to cook or to be at her apartment, sometimes she would slip into the Castro Theatre and crunch popcorn and watch old movies, letting her mind move away from crying children and the hard, unexplainable reality that she had no friends, no one to love. When the movie came to an end, she would often end up at A Different Light Bookstore, and she would search for any new lesbian authors that had surfaced lately. She would then walk home, often around midnight, listening to the tap of her footsteps on the sidewalk. While she experienced a comforting feeling in San Francisco and its normalizing of differences, still she felt a nagging sensation to leave the city, to venture into a rather intangible outer world—somewhere that resonated with her dreaminess—perhaps with a person who could meet her deepest callings.

Underneath this desire, though, she felt a provincial ineptness that stifled her. Her naivete seemed to kill every adventurous idea that popped into her brain.

One Saturday she walked over to the Mission District, to Valencia Street, where the smells of garlic, cumin, jalapeño, and cilantro wafted in the air. She entered the iconic Artemis Café, where she had once been part of a coming-out group led by a woman named Dolly. It was her first formal entrance into the world of being gay, and when it ended a few months later, she expected entire worlds to open to her. Instead, it fueled the sting inside her, a loneliness, an awkwardness with life itself.

One of the "graduation" exercises was to go to a lesbian bar. She tried this with her fellow coming-out colleagues, and as she sat at the bar that evening and looked around, she felt a weird sensation that *they* knew what they were doing, while she had not the foggiest idea how to drink, dance, pick up women, or even talk. Without saying goodbye to anyone from her group, she sulked out into the world of her solo travels, through the city that, despite feeling like home, left her wanting something more.

She ended up at one of her favorite cafés, the Dancing Monkey. She ordered a café au lait. She let the thick cream and strong coffee dance inside her, as they happily did a rumba on her tongue and then descended to her stomach where, eventually, they would create havoc and entirely terminate her café au lait urgings. For now, though, her body satiated, Marlene went to the restroom and looked over the bulletin board in the hallway to the entrance of the toilets. She did not need a roommate, an apartment, or a job. She did not need a massage or someone to clean up after her. The postings were all the same. New, though, since her last visit, was a flyer, handwritten in English with European handwriting, which announced a lesbian bed-and-breakfast in Paris. She read it over three times and then took it down. Back at her table, she quickly wrote down the phone number and other details, and then she put the flyer back up on the bulletin board. With the kind of smile that had not appeared on her face for ages, she made her way home. Her hands trembled on the receiver of her phone as she mouthed the French words in her mind and pressed the buttons, all eleven of them.

CHAPTER TWO

Isère, France

1985

Thérèse Aguillon stared at the neighboring cows and the rain and listened to one of Beethoven's compositions for *quatuor à cordes* on Radio France. She put another log on the fire and found a thick scarf to wrap around her neck. In her old farmhouse in the small town of Montbonnot, in the Isère region of France, ten kilometers outside Grenoble, she pondered the last eight hours. She was a psychiatrist with an office in Grenoble, where every day she received a cast of characters, various sorts of people who needed someone to listen to them, to help them ease their way through the tangled fibers of life. Her cases were challenging, most of them recent releases from the nearby psychiatric hospital, and they were, as a result, quite shaky in managing the world and in finding a path that would serve them and remove the obstacles they faced. Thérèse was good at this, however. Her patients often told her they felt heard and understood. Many of them would tell her this was the first time in their lives this occurred. Despite her tiny frame, Thérèse indeed had a huge heart that had, over the years, proved to be exceptionally compassionate. She was enthusiastic about her work and intense in her desire to help troubled people, to understand the deeper aspects of humanity.

She understood madness. When Thérèse was a small child, her mother began a lifelong *pas de deux* with this malady. Throughout Thérèse's youth, her mother had been in and out of hospitals until the day she took her life, when Thérèse was twenty-one years old, and still ensconced in her studies in Psychiatry at the University of Grenoble. After her mother's death, Thérèse became enmeshed in grief. A deep, hollow pit often consumed her, one that would persist for decades and that would continually plague her in everything that had to do with love and attachment.

On this rainy night, she had, as she often did, an orchestra of voices in her head. Her patients of the day resonated in her conscious mind. Their nuanced soliloquies had serenaded her as the windshield wipers swept back and forth, a defining rhythm that calmed her on her drive home. She had chosen to live out in the country, at the foot of the Alps. She discovered after her mother had passed that the mountains gave her an infinite spaciousness in which to breathe and to replenish her soul. Once she left the main road through town, she loved maneuvering her car along the tiniest of roads, up to the top of her property overlooking the Belledonne mountain range. After she parked her car, she had to walk up a short dirt path to get to her front door. Once inside, she would let out a sigh and breathe in the age of the building, a hundred-year-old structure that once belonged to a family of shepherds. When the elderly couple had died, the children had not wanted anything to do with the isolated home and sold both it and the sheep to Thérèse, who was just out of medical school and in desperate need of a home that bathed itself in the calm of nature. She promptly sold the sheep, as she knew she would not have the time to tend to the animals. She used the proceeds to make upgrades on the simple house. Her main priorities were to install an inside toilet and shower.

As the rain pelleted the windows, her eyes stared into the blur of grays outside. The voices of her patients no longer lingered, and her thoughts now were only her own. The andante movement from the radio, the two violins, viola, and cello, diminished the intensity of the day. She imagined a concert hall, a grand one, and herself in the audience. Her mother had wanted her oldest daughter to become a musician or, if not, a luthier, someone who created violins and cellos. She wanted the first child that came from her loins to create music in a way that had not been possible for her because of her family's poverty. Thérèse never felt that she had the gift to be a musician, however, and her hands did not seem to be created to make instruments. While these realizations were a grand disappointment to her mother, Thérèse would always have inside her a fascination and a love of music.

"I don't understand why you can't play the violin," her mother would often say.

"I don't have the right hands, Maman."

"That's ridiculous. What do you mean?"

"Look at them. They are tiny. It's like God forgot that hands are supposed to be proportionate to the arms." She always tried to laugh her way out of these perpetual dead-end conversations with her mother.

"Well, then, make violins. Hands can be any size for that trade."

Her mother would persist, always filling in the gaps where humor could not.

"Okay, I am not a hands person. Period." Thérèse tried to head for the door, change the subject, do anything but placate her mother.

"That's a euphemism for a lost soul. You are a lost soul, Thérèse, a grand disappointment. It is not worth living knowing I have a daughter who is such a failure at life."

The conversation would usually end there. Thérèse could never find the words to console her mother, not to mention herself.

Silence would ensue in the house until nighttime, when she would often hear her mother cry herself to sleep. Sometimes she would do the same in her own bed.

Once her mother died, Thérèse began to fervently listen to music. She thought it might bring her to that place of infinite connection with the soul of the woman who brought her into this world. Every evening, she listened to the radio. The sounds from the speakers made her feel that she was in the middle of a concert hall and the music was being played just for her.

On this rainy night, the rain and Beethoven did something to her. She imagined she was a witness to greatness in a grand concert hall, listening to the best musicians of Europe. Violins, violas, cellos, and basses flooded her ears as the transcendence of music transported her to an ethereal world.

I must get to Paris.

The voice inside her head was insistent.

CHAPTER THREE

San Francisco

1985

Marlene rubbed the backs of children who were rapidly falling asleep. The little ones always asked for her at nap time. Somehow, she knew just how to help each one relax the body, to enter the state of dreams. While her hands moved rhythmically back and forth, that day her mind was elsewhere, in the conversation, in French, she'd had just two days earlier. She had somehow produced the right words to ask about the Parisian bed-and-breakfast she had seen advertised in the bathroom hallway at the Artemis Café. On the phone, her voice shook and her brain floundered as she tried to get the words out to make the inquiry, her high school and college French courses clearly inadequate. As she spoke, however, she felt giddy.

As the children snored and the rain fell hard on the streets outside, a blustery winter wind accompanying the pelleting sounds, Marlene's thoughts tumbled to her actions: she had booked a flight to Paris in one month's time, during the closure of the school for winter break.

She looked around the room. All the children were fast asleep; their sleep sounds and drool drizzled the room with moisture and an audible hum. The teacher's aide entered and nodded, signaling to Marlene that it was time for her break. Quietly exiting the nap room, she threw on her coat and boots and ventured outside into the storm, letting the cold raindrops pound mercilessly on her oversized umbrella. She jumped over puddles and pranced down the sidewalk, ignoring the sour expressions of the occasional passerby. She felt like she was holding a secret deep inside. Now she had a destination, somewhere to go that deepened all her longings, something that was just hers. She was now ready to be the traveler, ready to escape and land on a part of the earth that she had only dreamed of.

Marlene felt a bit deranged in her new excitement. She was a calm, stoic person who didn't get excited about very much, and so her enthusiasm about her new plan took her by surprise. Even though she was the one who'd instigated it.

Marlene ended up at Café aux Îles, her favorite, near the corner of Duboce Street and Noe, hidden away in the back of a small alley. She sat at her favorite table by the window, looked out at the rain, and sipped her bowl of coffee with milk. She wondered if it tasted this delicious in Paris. Better, she thought. *I shall spend every day drinking café au lait, finding cafés every hour in which I can indulge myself.* A mini-symphony began to swell within her, a rhapsody of dreaminess, as her brain flitted from one desire to another. *Paris. How can one city carry with it such a sense of majesty, of transformation, of magic intertwined in just the word itself? Look at me, I'm seduced already, and I'm not even there yet. I, the fool...* With that declaration, she looked at her watch and realized she had only five minutes to walk back to work when it would normally take fifteen. She threw herself out into the streets, laughing, crazed, the caffeine and her excitement enough to fill the contours of the city that she was soon to leave.

CHAPTER FOUR

Thérèse wept as the sopranos and baritones exchanged angelic voices, Beethoven's genius in his opera *Fidelio* magnified by the transcendent acoustics at the Opéra Royale du Chateau de Versailles. She stared at the cellos and now wished more than anything that she had learned to play. The bow arms of the musicians mesmerized her, how they lucidly seemed to embrace the strings, expressing what only the soul can, those moments of the divine in the act of love and devotion. Her tears fell relentlessly down her cheeks and cascaded to her lap as she experienced grief and then a kind of resurrection, as she witnessed greatness in the sounds that emanated from the entire orchestra, the chorus, melodies that sang to her, seemingly to her alone, and that praised a god, a divine being, transcending the weaknesses, the fallacies of the human existence. Her body did not flinch, not even her eyes blinked as she sat on the edge of her cushioned chair, her concert ticket clutched in her left hand, her program in her right. The magnificence of this resplendently ornate eighteenth-century concert hall, the elegant, gilded architecture accentuated the brilliance of the sounds that emanated around her. While the concert hall was full, Thérèse noticed no one. She let herself be transported by the music. She was famished. Her brain seemed to gallop like an unbridled horse; a fervent passion grabbed hold of her in that moment of voluptuous pleasure. At the end of each passage, she sat back and sighed.

There was no intermission, and when the opera was finished, when the curtain ceased its ascents and descents, when all the applause waned to a quiet morsel, Thérèse, wiping her face, turned her head to the right and noticed there was a woman next to her clapping still, but mostly gazing at her. The woman's dark eyes were piercing; her dimples creased in such a way that Thérèse felt her knees grow weak from the quick glance, the gaze that might have lasted two seconds but felt like a lifetime. She noticed that she was panting and tried to disguise that reaction as she kept clapping, but then she felt like a fool and quickly stared at the floor and gathered her scattered thoughts. Her hands became quiet as her words tumbled out.

"C'etait un oeuvre d'un génie, un magicien, voyez-vous? C'etait comme une résurrection, une épiphanie…ahhh…cette beauté. Elle évoque les dieux, d'un monde si pur."

Thérèse looked at the concert hall, the now empty seats, and then she stared at the woman who had been invisible to her just moments before. Her eyes hinted at a desperation to connect. She followed the curve of her hair that flowed around her shoulders and down her back. Every bit of her wanted to kiss this woman. The more she stared, the more she realized that this was the woman she had been waiting for all those years she had been alone.

Marlene looked at Thérèse but said nothing. She was trying to convey something, but her words seemed stuck in her throat.

Thérèse tried again. *"La musique…"* Her words trailed off as the urge to kiss Marlene became stronger. She sensed a cloud had emerged in the space where all was silent. The auditorium was now empty, and the usher, who had just discovered them, came to their box and demanded they leave the hall at once.

* * *

Marlene did not understand a word Thérèse said. Before the usher arrived, she had felt heat in her neck that began to consume her. At first, when she looked in Thérèse's eyes, sensations flooded her she had never experienced, a palpable longing. Thérèse's hand was close to hers. She looked down and almost put hers in it. Then a voice invaded her brain, that of her own mother. "*You will never find someone to love, Marlene…*" She gulped. She tried to push the voice away. She began to sweat profusely as the image of her deceased mother flooded her, the woman who had made her own daughter a scapegoat for her own tragedies. She felt her strength wane. A cloud passed over her mind and body, and all she could do was gather her coat in her arms. She looked up at Thérèse and managed a meek smile as she walked away.

Her numbness followed her like a maimed ghost as she approached the train station and boarded the train that would take her back to her lesbian bed-and-breakfast.

* * *

Thérèse secretly followed and climbed onto the same train, several cars back. She longed to sit next to Marlene, the one who had made her shake inside. A desperation filled her as she thought about trying to find her on the train. She hesitated, sensing that this woman who had been sitting next to her during the entire concert was not interested in having a conversation. *Why did she get up and leave, after that piercing gaze?* She found Marlene's face intriguing. She imagined tracing the lines of it with her fingertips. *Did she speak another language? Perhaps that gaze was a fleeting moment in her life, something to run from.* She thought of her lips that curved and flowed like a goddess on a mountain peak, a place she longed to explore. With a sullen look on her face, Thérèse sank into her seat and stared into the blackness of the night.

She tried to divert her thoughts from Marlene to the concert, her mind still full of the opera. It was this she also longed for: music, voices and instruments that pierced into the depths of her, filling spaces in her too long empty soul. This is what her mother had wanted for her, she realized, as she felt tears well up. Thérèse wanted to be able to transcend life and its bleakness through music. She wanted to create something beautiful from a primitive place in her brain. Thérèse realized that during most of the concert she had stared at the cello section, loving how the musicians' arms embraced the instruments. *Ah, to be connected to the cello*, she thought, *would be a dream fulfilled.* She closed her eyes, letting the notes, float through her dreamy state. As the train sped along, whisking itself from the country to the suburban span of Paris, sleep claimed her body, letting the conscious and the un-conscious dreams mingle into a translucent web of beauty that surrounded her.

CHAPTER FIVE

Marlene lay down in her tiny bed and closed her eyes, but sleep was elusive. Images of Thérèse nagged at her. With her small, bony frame, she was not particularly beautiful, but there was something about her eyes that drew her in. It was like she saw people, heard their desires, understood them through a quick glance. She wanted to go back and do it all over again. She wanted desperately to have responded to this woman, to have held her hand, to have let the confusing and consuming heat take its own course. She cursed her ignorance of French. When Thérèse spoke, it sounded so beautiful, the cadences like a poem. Marlene wondered what the Frenchwoman had said. She wondered what her hand felt like. She wondered what Thérèse's lips would feel like on hers.

She cursed her mother. She cursed her own life. She cried for what seemed like hours. Somewhere amid the tears, sleep overcame her.

* * *

Marlene looked at the clock. It was noon already; she had slept half the day away. At one point in the early morning, she had woken up to quiet voices in the room. She heard only English, and US English at that. The sound of her mother tongue annoyed her, and she wanted to flee from her own accent, from those around her who spoke the same English that she had been born with. She was surprised that all the women in the B and B were Americans. Many were not even lesbians, she thought, as they were whispering about the French men they had met that they wanted to sleep with. She then drifted back to a jet-lagged, heavy sleep.

The *auberge* was quiet and empty when she finally got out of bed and listened to a distant church bell that rang two times. She made herself a *tartine* and poured herself a steaming bowl of coffee to which she added a nice blend of milk. As the fresh jam and butter and coffee slid tenderly down her throat, she stared out the window at the grayish skies. *It looks like it might be a rainy afternoon in Paris. A perfect day to see art, to immerse myself in paintings and sculptures, to absorb all that is French into my veins.*

As she gazed out at a darkened sky, she thought of Thérèse, the music, the concert hall, Versailles. She let these images coalesce in front of her and sink into an amorphous hole. She had arrived in Paris just the day before. Immediately she had felt an overwhelming explosion in all her senses. She knew she was experiencing a kind of birth of something inside her that shook her up, that ignited a part of her that she had never known. She felt like she wanted to taste Paris; she wanted to listen to its sounds, to revel in its sheer wonderment, its age, and its self-conscious beauty. Being in Paris, she decided, was like being in a dream where you wanted to touch everything, smell everything, and let the aesthetics of the city encompass you. That first day the sounds of French had shimmied all around her as she sat in cafés and listened to people chat. The up-and-down musicality of the language made her euphoric.

She wanted more. In one of the first cafés that she discovered, she saw a poster for a concert that evening in Versailles. Later that day she found a tourist information booth and asked the woman behind the counter how to get there. Within the hour she was on the train. She pranced around the gardens and imagined the folly of Marie Antoinette, her excess, the endless fantasy of her whims. The castle itself was a place of gilded overzealousness. When finally, she sat down in her seat in the pristinely ornate concert hall, she looked around her with even more hunger. She wanted the music to feed her, to take her mind into an era of timeless beauty, into a musical lexicon that challenged her simple brain. She did not know much about classical music. Beethoven was to her a man who became Deaf and wrote music, yet she knew nothing about his work. When the concert began, the first notes drifting through the air resonated with her desire for beauty. When the violins and cellos sang to each other, one instrument with the next, first quietly, then with more bravado, Marlene experienced a marriage of sounds, what she imagined was lovemaking on a musical level. She could hardly put into words what she had experienced, even in English; it seemed to her an experience that went far beyond language itself.

As her thoughts slowed, as the rain fell harder on the pavement below the B and B, her mind drifted to one last image: Thérèse. Her voice was so passionate, her language so melodic, sensuous in its revelry in all things beautiful. She would do anything to be able to see her again, to gather enough courage to say anything; even one word, *Merci*, would be enough. She again cursed her one chance at connection with someone who had made Paris her lover, just as she was beginning to do.

When she had gotten on the train afterward, everything had felt like one grand blur. She had closed her eyes, and when they opened again, she was at Gare Montparnasse. She slipped into the folds of the Metro station to get to the next train. It was midnight and musicians were still playing as she boarded her next train. She got off at Bir-Hakeim and decided to walk to her neighborhood, rather than get on another train to La Muette, the station nearest her bed-and-breakfast.

It had turned into a beautiful night, crisp with the winter wind, a cloudless sky. The lights of *La tour Eiffel* illuminated the city. Marlene stood silently under a streetlight and took it all in. She felt calmed by the iron-and-lace lady that illuminated this city of magic and splendor. She sighed. She imagined Thérèse, her arms around her.

I will never forget her. She will become emblematic of my love affair with all that is Paris.

CHAPTER SIX

Thérèse walked brazenly through the Marais, the cobblestones round and smooth under her feet. It was around midnight, yet she did not heed the time. Her favorite café, La Muse, was open, and she sat down and ordered a glass of wine. Sitting alone next to the window, she watched a quiet street, yet around her, in the city that enveloped her, there was always sound. Paris never slept, and Thérèse loved that. When she visited, she enjoyed staying at her friend's apartment when she was away. She never slept during these occasional visits because she loved to throw her structured life out the window. Yet even in Paris, her solitary life surrounded her. Sometimes she wondered if this habit would ever change. Being alone had become so comfortable for her. She sipped her wine and swirled the acidity around her tongue. She thought of Marlene. In quiet moments, she wondered what it would be like to have someone to love. When she allowed her feelings to surface, she realized she was desperate for it.

She reviewed the events of the day and landed once again on the softness of Marlene's face, her dark, piercing eyes. She remembered how her own body had weakened. As the wine slid comfortably down her throat, she saw her own reflection, as if she were staring at herself naked in a mirror in that café. She saw her own loneliness and gasped. She glanced around the room and stared at the door, hoping that Marlene would step inside at precisely the same moment she had looked over. She imagined their locked gaze, their friendship sealed for life.

A couple walked in, hand in hand. They laughed. They were obviously in love. It accentuated Thérèse's solitude as she ordered another glass of wine.

She turned her head to the wall across from her, where a poster caught her attention, in French.

"We, here in the Marais, connect deeply with one another as we support and help each other in all ways. The most despicable war in our times ended more than forty years ago. It is now that we are in the process of finding musical instruments that were mercilessly taken from our families before they were shoved in cattle cars bound for concentration camps. Many of you have heard of the famous ERR—Einsatzstab Reichleiter Rosenberg, a dedicated team, calling themselves the Sonderstab Musik (Music Commando), who were sent to France beginning in the early 1940's to gather up as many musical instruments that they could find, all belonging to individuals who fell under anti-Semitic laws. Most of the instruments they looked for had completely vanished, many of which were sent away to Germany, destroyed in the Blitz or burnt in the camps. Particularly noteworthy is our search for looted violins and violincellos, some that were of great monetary value, and others that were cherished in our family's sentimental heirlooms. Our aim is to retrieve these instruments, and to return them to the families that are the rightful owners. We shall start in a nationwide search, and then extend across Europe and even overseas, keeping our mission alive for as long as it takes. If you are interested in being a part of this monumental project, please contact The Association of Looted Music, attention Jakub Bernovitch, 28 place des Vosges 75004 Paris. Phone number 33(0) 1 04 58 88 18.

Thérèse read the flyer over and over. She cried. She copied down the number, left the café, and silently walked through the streets of the Marais. Everything felt different now, these streets where thousands of Jews were carted away, their wails stifled in the nights of July 16–17, 1942, as they were herded by the Vichy police to the Vélodrome d'Hiver, steps away from the Bir-Hakeim Bridge overlooking the Eiffel Tower.

For much of her life, Thérèse had been infatuated with this city, drawn into a seductive embrace. In the space of five minutes, after having read the flyer, she felt a part of herself launch into a different kind of love, the kind that nourishes others, that lives in the space of the heart, its precious and infinite folds. Her thoughts tumbled now through her brain, the parts of the cerebral cortex that processes old wounds. Music had been her calling ever since her mother wished it so, even before that, for her mother wanted to be that musician herself. Thérèse steadfastly walked up the rue de Turennes, her steps firm, her heart glued to the complicated notion that she loved her country, a love mingled with disgust at how her country had treated Semitic people in a time where everyone needed love. She heard those violins and cellos in her head, played that evening at Versailles, and imagined them played by mangled hands as their bodies fell limp, burned in the gas chambers.

She wanted to scream, there after midnight in the now quiet streets.

Instead, she sat on the bed in her friend's apartment and grasped the piece of paper with the phone number of Monsieur Bernovitch, whom she would call that next morning.

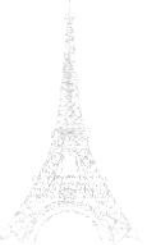

CHAPTER SEVEN

Marlene sat on the Métro, headed to the Musée d'Orsay. She looked around. In the seat across from her was a young mother holding a baby fast asleep. The mother had fair skin, and the infant was much darker. Marlene knew staring was rude, yet she could not lift her gaze from this scene, from the adoration of this woman toward the being that she held so lovingly in her arms. Every day at work, Marlene had witnessed this bonding, this attachment between mother and baby. She often wondered what this felt like.

As the train moved through the bowels of Paris, the sovereign, embellished world of the underground, Marlene's perceptions of what she saw in life became altered. Something that was once commonplace transformed itself during her Parisian escape. Like Proust dipping his madeleine into a steaming cup of tea, whereupon something extraordinary transpires, Marlene felt herself shudder. She knew that nothing would ever be the same again in her life.

"No sooner had the warm liquid mixed with the crumbs touched my palate than a shudder ran through me, and I stopped, intent upon the extraordinary thing that was happening to me."

She felt something dislodge in her heart. Tears streamed down her face as she descended from the train and ascended to the streets of Paris, where a gentle rain awaited her.

She was not ready to enter the museum as she walked through

the Tuileries. For a moment, she thought she was the only one there, and she felt the cold and the rain hit her cheeks, her hair now a glistening, moistened mass of curls as the barren trees surrounded her, the winter foliage asleep and turned inward. She imagined these gardens in full bloom, and though she knew as little about art as she knew about music, what would call to her later that afternoon would be Manet's painting, *Music in the Tuileries*, on loan from the National Gallery in London. Prior to looking at the painting in the gallery, she had a vision in her head that resembled a party, a huge garden party with an abundance of life from another era. She further imagined herself there, a baby in her arms, yes, an infant, her child, and she imagined the smiles on both their faces, hers and her daughter's.

It was in that moment, where an imaginary sun and a spring full of nascent life mingled with the hibernating, wintry folds of her present condition, that Marlene knew.

When I return to the US, I am going to begin the process of adopting a child, a daughter.

Dripping rain and giddy from her musings outside, she entered the museum. While Impressionist masterpieces surrounded her, her eyes fixed on only one theme: mothers and daughters. Mary Cassatt and Berthe Morisot stood out for her, and not ever having seen their paintings, she stood in front of them and sighed. She felt their brilliance, but mostly she resonated with something inside her that now screamed out. In each of these tableaux there was love, devotion, and the maternal instinct, as represented in the light-filled images, the softness in the gaze, the return to something that went far beyond self to another being. As Marlene stared for hours at these paintings, going back and forth among them, something monumental occurred inside her. She felt akin to a maturing plant, a bud pushing through hardened masses of an ego-driven self, to a place of something sublime, a transformation of what she knew of herself to something much more altruistic in nature. She perused a few of Renoir's depictions of mothers and children and found them all stilted, a disconnection between the infant and its mother. She hungrily returned to Cassatt and Morisot, as she would, in her mind in years to come, return to those two paintings. In the expressions of tenderness she had found there, the part of her that longed for such an experience found inspiration, and she was ready for such an event in her life.

When she left the museum, the rain now over and the weak sun beginning to peek through, she felt a resurgence of passion in her surroundings, a lust for more, her blood a pulsing sensation, a vital essence that animated her steps. She felt her heart beating with longing to nourish the life of someone who was, at that exact moment, in the very act of conception. She imagined that somewhere in the world, in the bed of someone she would never know, was the very beginning of a life that she would come to know. With that thought in her mind, her steps became light and took her through neighborhood after neighborhood. Paris was cementing her newly forming self.

As she looked up and all around, the age of everything mixed with grace, she came to realize that Paris was her lover because she had made it so, because the infinite particles of who she was resonated on a deep level with the city, its identity, now and over time. She had never experienced this sensation before and never would again, anywhere else.

She arrived at the rue de Turennes, in the heart of the Marais, and sat down at a café called La Muse. As the voice of Édith Piaf serenaded the room with "La Vie en Rose," she sipped a glass of wine and let the fragrance swirl over her tongue.

She came to realize then that growing up and discovering who you are often proceeded leaving home, finding a place in the world that resonated.

She finished her glass of wine and strolled in a happy delirium
through the Marais to the Saint-Paul Métro station. She did not
know yet where she would disembark. When the train stopped at
Châtelet, she instinctively got off and walked across the Seine, feeling the cool air bathe her face. When she arrived at Notre Dame,
she gawked at the gargoyles that jutted out from each corner of
the exterior of the iconic cathedral. She chuckled to herself as she
remembered a poem she once read in a magazine. She had held
these words in her brain for a dozen years: "When gargoyles dog
your every step, still you walk this world alone."

*Maybe now, finally, I will no longer walk this world alone, and
maybe now, no longer will I have such gargoyles.*

PART TWO

Les Enfants

Thérèse sat down in the train and stared out the window. She watched her country speed by as if she were looking through a fast-motion camera. There were endless agricultural fields, winter life dormant as dark clouds permeated the sky, shades of green and gray accentuating the quiet of the season. In that translucent state of mindlessness, she closed her eyes and let the past few days meld into a diffuse mélange of experiences, memories, and life-changing events.

Just that morning she had had a meeting at the Place des Vosges. She had looked straight in the eyes of Monsieur Bernovitch as he spoke. Tears fell gently from his face.

"My entire family died in the gas chambers. I was the only one who managed to survive the atrocities. I am from a family of musicians, all string players, and my earliest memories centered around music. There was always music at home, always partitas, concertos, and duets that my parents played as I ambled around in diapers in the apartment. What they taught me was that music transcends the bad, except when it did not. All the family instruments stayed behind when the Nazis carted us away to the Vélodrome, en route to Auschwitz."

He was silent then, staring at the mezuzah on the doorframe of the café.

"Somehow, I survived. Somehow, those harrowing moments

became part of my past. I returned, tentatively, to Paris. I was put in an orphanage, and my dreams all led to those instruments that my parents had hidden under the bed. I continued to replay the loud knock on the door, a sound that would always accentuate the roar in my little toddler ears."

He paused again, watching the rain outside.

"When eventually I left the orphanage and was adopted by a family, those dreams continued. They continued into my adolescence and adulthood, while I obtained a degree in music at the Sorbonne and earned the position of section leader, first cellist with L'Orchestre National de France. Finally, one day, in the middle of rehearsal, at a point in my life where those dreams had grown to disproportionate heights, it finally dawned on me what to do. As I plowed through the section rehearsal, listening to the other cellists with one ear, with the other I heard my parents, their wistful notes, and as those sounds gelled in one part of my brain, the idea for the Association of Looted Music arose in the other."

"So, what is your interest in this project, Madame Aguillon?" he asked when he finished his story. "Your name is not of Jewish origin."

"No, I'm not Jewish." She looked away from his gaze for a second and gathered her thoughts. "Something resonated in me when I saw the flyer last night. I cannot exactly describe it. Something deeply embedded in me called out. Was it my dead mother's wish for me to be a musician? Then I realized it was more. Was it the calling I felt to do what I can to make right the vile wrongs committed by the Vichy government, manipulated by the Germans? Was it just part of my nature to help others, to create sanity in a world that is so often insane? I love my country, and I hate when others are excluded, tormented, killed, and pulled away from what is so meaningful for them. France is a country of tolerance, of acceptance, a democracy that is undivided. What can we, as

Frenchmen and Frenchwomen do, all of us, to reconcile, to bring back justice, to bring back music, the purest art form on this planet? When I heard your story, I felt even more pulled in this direction, as a mother feels the pull toward her own child, that assiduous thread leading to a protected place of redemption, that healing balm in a shattered world. I knew I needed to spend this portion of my life looking for instruments, helping to return them to their rightful owners."

Thérèse stopped there; she was visibly shaking as Monsieur Bernovitch held her hand and cried with her.

"I am thinking of Brahms's *Symphony No. 3*. Do you know that piece?" he asked, tenderness in his eyes.

"Very well." She sat silently and conjured up the second movement. She heard in her head the winds and the strings converse in tones that only made the listener cry. "It expresses what we are talking about."

"Do you have the second movement, the Andante, in your head?'

"Completely. The English horn calls out for peace toward the end. The loving exchange between the strings and the winds. The theme of the cellos, mirrored by the rest of the orchestra, sends shivers up one's spine. It makes me see, in my mind, visions of every one of those instruments. We absolutely must find them."

"And at the very end, the French horn recreates the mood, doesn't it?" he said with fervor. "Every instrument in the orchestra repeats this theme. It is a collective plea, as you say, this finding redemption, if this is even possible, but it's the plea for unity, for love on this planet, for the beauty of music."

They continued to hold each other's hands, a Jew and a Gentile, understanding that through music, somehow healing happens.

"I would love to have your help, Madame Aguillon. We will talk next week by phone with the specifics." Despite the pathos of his life, his eyes twinkled, and as he shook her hand goodbye, she looked in his eyes and saw and felt the urgency of this meeting, this project, music underscoring it all.

"And please call me Jakub," he added.

CHAPTER NINE

Marlene crouched over a sleeping child and looked around the room at the others who were squirming, waiting for a back rub. She got up, whispered to the next child that it was time to begin to relax the body, to let the mind be quiet. She gently put her hand on the tiny back of the three-year-old and soothed this tightly wound body. Enya's voice serenaded the room, as Marlene's mind drifted back to Paris. She felt like she was still there, connected to a transcendence in herself, movement toward her inner vision.

"So…our little traveler, tell us all about Paris," her colleague and favorite fellow teacher Juanita asked in the break room the day she got back.

"Wonderful!"

"Is that all you're going to tell us? Did you meeeeeeet anyone?" Juanita had a smirk on her face.

"I ate tons of croissants, drank lots of café au laits, saw lots of art, listened to beautiful music…"

"OK. That's nice. So why do you have a glow on your face? Did you fall in love, darling?"

"How about if I tell you in a bit? I am still working through some things."

"Not good enough. Secrets kept here." Juanita pointed to her heart as she motioned to her sealed lips.

Marlene looked around to make sure no one was listening. Then, in a whisper, she told her colleague about her love affair with Paris, her encounter with Thérèse, her desire to become a mother, and how she stared for an hour at Berthe Morisot's *The Cradle.*

"Oh my god, girl, you had a time!"

"I guess I did…"

"Good for you, sweetie."

Marlene's break was over, and she had to help the children wake up from their naps.

"More later?"

"Sure."

Marlene walked away with a smile on her face. What she did not say was that she had found the phone number of the central adoption agency in San Francisco and had, earlier that week, met with one of the counselors.

"This is confidential information, Marlene," the counselor had whispered, and then quietly shut the door to her office. She looked seriously at Marlene, who had just described her decision to adopt a child from another country, preferably a girl.

"We have been privy to some scandalous information, which hasn't yet been brought to the attention of the public," she continued, her tone serious.

"In Romania, the situation is bleak. The beginning of the fall of Ceausescu's communist dictatorship has revealed extreme corruption. Everywhere, authorities are finding children whose parents have abandoned them in the streets. They send them to orphanages, where the children undergo horrific abuse. Many of these children have profound physical and psychological disabilities and deformities because of a decrepit medical system. I believe this will be the beginning of mass adoptions, and I predict they are going to be gouging rich Americans and Europeans. These children will most probably require expensive medical interventions that, of course, the Romanian government would never pay for."

The counselor looked even more serious. "I have connections, Marlene."

Marlene gulped. Fear enveloped her, yet underneath she felt a fervor to proceed, to let the counselor be her guide. She wanted desperately to forge a path toward the daughter who was waiting for her, who needed her most.

CHAPTER TEN

Thérèse held the phone in her hand and cradled it like a treasure. After talking with Jakub, she now stared at the snow that fell gently outside, the lacy white that decorated the hillsides and embellished the earth. She grabbed her coat and her keys and put a cassette of Bach partitas in the cassette deck of her car; then she slowly headed out of her snow-covered driveway onto the main road into Grenoble. On this Saturday, there was no one on the road, which normally would have been filled with cars heading into the city. Her mind centered on the phone conversation, the words, freshly painted in her brain, propelling her into this next phase of her life.

"This will take a bit of sleuthing, Madame, a passion for discovery. Do you have that in you?" he'd asked.

Thérèse had smiled at that question. As a psychiatrist, every day she was a sleuth. Rarely would her clients spell out their insights and hand them to her on a silver platter. No, it was the careful art of intrigue that propelled her, the subtle cues of human existence that she had learned to rely on. Over the years, she had perfected the skill of asking pertinent questions as well as listening to and observing the answers. She had also become a teacher of sleuthing, letting her patients become impassioned by their own discoveries of themselves, which would allow them to heal from all the wounds that had erupted during their lives.

"I have become a master of sleuthing," Thérèse responded, laughing. "It gives me immense pleasure to find things out of obscurity, the needles in the haystacks."

"Indeed." Jakub laughed too, a full belly laugh. "I am inspired by you, Madame." He ventured forward. "So, what region are you in, is that Isère?"

"Yes."

"Well, let's start off with something local for you, let you ease into this work, shall we?"

"Fabulous! What did you have in mind?"

"Well, I have recently received a phone call from a thrift shop in Grenoble that just received a violin from an unnamed gentleman who walked in. He said his mother had bought it right after the war, and he had no use for it. Could you please check this out today before it is gone? Pay what you can for it. We can reimburse you for anything you buy. The process works this way: we buy countless instruments from thrift stores and the like, and if we indeed decide that this instrument does not belong to anyone who is looking for it, then we sell it at auction. We have an expert, here in Paris, who looks at and evaluates each instrument that is brought in. I am connected to thrift shops everywhere, and they know my organization will pay them a good price. In addition, we need to work fast, as the shop owners, in general, will not hold an instrument for more than twenty-four hours. They feel like they are doing us a service for even this much. Do you think you could do this today?"

Thérèse looked at the snow that was falling steadily.

"Absolutely," she responded. "I shall get on the road straightaway."

"Perfect. Phone me when you get back with the instrument and describe it to me. I shall be in the office until 7 p.m."

Thérèse held the phone and listened to the *click* as the line disconnected. Her heart raced about as loudly as the howling wind of the oncoming blizzard.

On the bus ride back home, the adoption counselor's parting words rang out in her mind like French church bells on a Sunday.

"You must not tell a soul about this. At least not until we have the final paperwork. I am about to unlock what could be considered a guarded safe, and I need to do this with your pledge of confidence. Do I have that? Is this something that you really want to proceed with?" She looked straight into Marlene's eyes with a piercing gaze. Marlene stared back, her palms sweaty and her heart racing.

"Take a few days to think about this. Don't rush into anything this monumental. This child will be with you for the rest of your life, and you need to be completely resolved about your decision to adopt. I know your financial situation. We have just received a generous grant from an anonymous donor, a resident of San Francisco, and because of this, I will not charge you a penny. You will need to purchase your own airline ticket, however, round-trip for yourself and one-way for the child, but the agency will cover all adoption expenses, if indeed you decide you want to adopt. Any medical expenses—and most probably there will be sizable ones—will need to be covered by you and your insurance company. You can get medical insurance for your child through your employment. If you agree to the adoption, I will have you contact our pro bono legal expert regarding the process of becoming the child's legal guardian, so she is able to be covered under your insurance plan. Also, once we have finalized everything, you will need to then talk to your employer and book a flight no more than two weeks later. If you wait longer than that, you run the risk that the Romanian government would step in, which would abolish your chances through our agency. As I said earlier, there are strong predictions that these Romanian adoptions will become a national epidemic."

The counselor looked right into Marlene. "You really want this, don't you?"

"Yes, more than anything in the world."

"These issues are not daunting?"

"I'm not thinking about how daunting it is." She laughed. "I am thinking about the child. I feel as if she is waiting for me, in a destitute orphanage that she absolutely needs to leave. I have a home for her. I have a heart that is ready to love a child. She can be at my childcare center until she is old enough to go to school. I will always be there for her. I want this child so much, no matter what her disabilities are."

Marlene was shaking. Her own truth poured out of her, as she remembered Thérèse, as the Morisot painting swirled in her memories, light infused in the drapes, the mother and the child in a perfect bond. She longed for that connection with a child who needed her and who, she realized, she also needed.

"Give it a day to really think it over, Marlene. Think with all your senses open, including your rational mind. Call me tomorrow before 6 p.m. And then, if you are still as positive, we can sign preliminary papers on Thursday evening. How does that sound?"

Marlene nodded. Tears were stuck inside, waiting for release.

The counselor reached out her hand, and Marlene took it with both her hands and held it tightly.

She walked out of the office onto Market Street. The approaching storm had reached its height, and the winds whipped furiously around her, sending the season's lingering leaves in all directions. As she waited at the bus stop, thick raindrops began to fall, mercilessly shrouding all light, infinite amounts of water dispersed everywhere. By the time the bus arrived, she was soaked through, but she took no notice. She took the last seat on the bus and stared out at a world that now, in her mind, was an awaiting home to a child who would be hers, forever.

CHAPTER TWELVE

If Thérèse had turned on the radio in her car, she would have heard weather warnings for the region of Isère: 90 percent chance of whiteouts by 5 p.m. Announcements told drivers to stay off the roads from 4 p.m. on, except in emergencies. As Bach continued to serenade her, all she could think about was the violin. She was oblivious to the snow around her that swirled in a silent syncopation as her windshield wipers beat back and forth, a steady rhythm. Yet a muted concern for safety had her driving slowly into town, forced to not give in to her whims of sailing along an empty highway. In the back of her mind, she was happy she had put brand-new snow tires on her car a few months earlier. Her thoughts turned to the compelling image of the violin, possibly one of the cherished, lost instruments. She lunged her whole self into the world of the detective.

When she reached Grenoble, the winds were howling even louder and thrashing the snow this way and that. There were few people out, and stores were closing, if they had not already shut their doors for the day.

The store was on 68, avenue Raymond Cartier, Jakub had said, right around the corner from the city ice arena, where they'd staged all the Olympic figure-skating competitions in the 1968 Grenoble Winter Olympics. *I know that neighborhood.* It was where her younger sister Nicole used to take figure-skating lessons, week after week, until the day her beloved teacher died of a sudden heart attack. Racked by pain and grief, she had never again put on a pair of figure skates. That was the year after their mother had killed herself, when their father clumsily took on the role of parent for the two girls. After the death of the skating teacher, her younger sister had fallen completely apart, for this teacher had been like a surrogate mother to her. Shortly after the teacher's death, the doctors diagnosed her sister with a rare form of cancer. She was gone a month later.

As Thérèse's thick boots clamped onto the soft snow, buried memories of the ice arena and everything associated with it rose into her consciousness. She walked by the front door that had a closed sign on it and looked in, noting that nothing seemed to have changed in the twenty years since those days when her sister's skating kept their struggling family barely afloat. At that time all three of them had been stumbling toward an unknown destination, one of being lost. The teacher's face came into her mind. She'd had such a sweet, warm smile. She had told Thérèse that her baby sister had true talent as a figure skater and that she would undoubtedly go far, become another Peggy Fleming, she had said with a twinkle in her eye.

A few times Nicole had visited the teacher at her house, where she lived with her girlfriend in a clandestine lesbian relationship, Thérèse had suspected. When Nicole died, the girlfriend, a violin teacher, insisted on playing her violin at the funeral. There, in the tiny church at the foot of the Vercors mountain, as the snow fell—for it was a hard winter that year—she played Gluck's "Mélodie" from *Orfeo and Euridice*. She had played the same piece at her partner's funeral just a few months earlier. As Thérèse walked around the ice arena, snow cascading onto her head, wind whirling through her thick jacket, she recalled the violin that day, so many years back. Its lush sounds still resonated in her ears, reminding her of the hollowness of it all, the sudden death of her beloved little sister right after their mother's passing. She had felt so alone that day, as the last notes were played and silence filled the church, echoing her grief. The Alps had soared around them. She took a deep breath and felt the cold in her nostrils as she came back to the present. It felt so long ago, yet not, as the sound of that violin still resounded in her brain.

Thérèse approached the storefront of 68, avenue Raymond Cartier. She focused on the violin of twenty years ago as she tried the door and found it locked. Suddenly, her mind shifted to the present, and the urgency of getting inside flooded her. She banged on the door, her hard fists knocking senselessly, reflecting her anxiety, anger, and grief.

Damn it. Why did my sister have to die? Why did all those violin owners have to be murdered? I shouldn't even be doing this project. It should not have happened, that war, Hitler, and why is it snowing now; the store should be open! She banged some more; this time her rage overtook her and took away all reason. She had survived all those years on the premise that the rational mind surpassed all. The world, hers, and the world around her had been knocked senseless, and she had to survive. She would listen to others express their pain, but she, no, she would never. As she stood at the door to the shop, she looked in and saw a dim light in the back. She banged louder; this time she pleaded, the desperate woman she had become.

This violin is my salvation, and I must have it. I need to get home with this instrument in my arms.

She did not recognize her own derangement. She was usually the calm one, the one with not the slightest hint of madness. She suddenly became wrapped in a frenzied state. She shuddered, feeling invaded by her mother's rage with the world. Teetering from this realization, she noticed the dim light in the back of the store become brighter. A darkened shape ventured toward the front door of the shop. A little man, not more than five feet, pushed open the drape. He pointed up at the sky as he told her firmly the shop was closed.

"Yes, yes, I know it's snowing, but there is a violin you have in your store, and I need to have it now!" Thérèse was yelling, partly to be heard through the closed door, and partly because her voice could not stop yelling, as if she had needed to yell all her life and this was the one moment where it exploded outward.

"*Demain*," he retorted, as he began to walk away.

"I have a great sum of money to pay you for it. Please let me in!"

The shop owner looked at her with a gruff expression, as if he was pretending that he was doing her a great service.

What an act. I am sure visions of francs are the only ones passing through his head.

He quickly unlocked the door and, without a word, brought out the violin, his expression still gruff and rushed.

Obviously wanting a quick sale. Probably his woman is waiting for him in the back.

He opened the case and displayed the violin for a second. He did not let Thérèse hold it. He then put it back in and snapped up the case.

"How much do you have?"

"How much are you asking for it?

"How much do you have?" he repeated, his voice insistent, impatient.

"Twenty-five hundred francs."

"Not enough." He took the case, walked toward the door, opened it, and showed her out.

"Wait. I have five hundred more francs in my other pocket."

"You said you had a lot of money. This is nothing." He motioned her to leave again.

"No, I need this violin, Monsieur. I can give you one thousand more on Monday, after the storm is over and I can get to the bank."

He nodded. He put out his hand, and Thérèse gave him all she had as he thrust the case into her arms. He then pushed her out the door, and slammed it shut behind her.

With the violin clutched to her belly, she walked briskly to her car. Her feet were heavy yet resilient on the thickly snowed walk, the pavement long since hidden away by winter's madness. Seeing the increasing accumulation of snow on the ground since she had parked, she quickly scraped off the newly fallen flakes on her windshield. She started the engine and gripped the steering wheel as she drove out of the neighborhood, through the abandoned streets of Grenoble, and onto the sheer white of the highway toward home.

As she headed away from the city, she glanced once at the violin beside her and smiled. Quickly this smile, however, vanished, as she saw flashing yellow lights at the side of the road, indicating there was a safety hazard information warning on the radio. She turned on the radio, wanting to hear Yehudi Menuhin, but instead, forced herself to listen to the reporting.

"Widespread blizzard and avalanche conditions have caused multiple road closures in the Isère region. Mandatory road closure on highway 7,500 meters after the Montbonnot exit until Saint-Ismier. Road closure on Highway…"

"Merde!" Thérèse screamed out. She turned off the metallic voice, put on Bach, and tried to will away her anger, the snow, and the rage that had infused her that day. Menuhin blithely soared through each passage, each note a jewel, a snowflake, an unencumbered morsel of brilliance. Part of Thérèse's brain followed each note. She felt pulled into his transcendent world where sorrow was only a dissipating feeling.

The yellow lights continued to blare even more succinctly as her knuckles turned as white as the snow outside. She could not see the sign for Montbonnot. She could not see much of anything and had no idea where she was on the highway until she arrived at a metal post that glared in front of her. It barricaded the road, and there was no viable way to maneuver her way around it.

"*Merde. Merde. Merde*," she screamed, her own voice echoing in the night. It was darker than dark, and not a soul was around. She parked her car on what she thought was the side of the road, pulled her scarf tighter around her neck, took the violin in one gloved hand, and held a tiny flashlight that had little battery left in the other. She then began the five-mile walk home.

Her feet trudged unwillingly on the unblemished snow. Each step forged a journey into her own angst, her life a morbid display of unresolved tragedy. As the snow relentlessly swirled around her, covering her hat, her hands, every one of her limbs with a cold and frenetic mix of ice and sorrow, she cried, she wailed, she bellowed out wordless epithets that sank into the depths of her heavy footsteps. Her boots barely gripped the slippery mass of white under her feet.

Step by step she ventured, not even sure if she was still on the highway. She thought she was, and she continued, yet her wailing did not cease. She relied on the strength of her body, the athletic musculature that she had produced as a swimmer, years ago. As the snow whipped through her, in her mind she put herself in an infinity pool. Her laps became one with her body, the endlessness of her strokes in the water, where nothing else seemed to matter. As she played this mind game, her footsteps in the snow became invisible to her conscious self; they just happened. The snowy crunch under her feet became her rhythm as her body moved onward, her gloved hand still clutching the violin. She gripped the leather handle even harder as Beethoven entered her conscious-ness, then Marlene, her gentle face. She felt a pulsing sensation, a heat run through her. Was it imaginary, she wondered, in this cold, to feel hot as she envisioned the woman next to her that evening? She wondered what Marlene was doing at that moment, wondered where she was, and the vision of her sweet face, the beauty that resounded around her that day stayed with Thérèse, as still she walked, as an effortlessness took over her promenade through the snow.

Like a mirage, the sign for St. Ismier loomed in front of her, mostly obscured now by the snow, except for the tops of the letters.

Thérèse heaved a sigh of relief as she got off the highway and followed the lights through town. She imagined people in their homes, warm and dry. The stores and restaurants were all dark, however, and her heart sank, for she longed for a cup of tea and a loan of a flashlight, as hers had the faintest light now and was mostly useless.

Hesitant to knock on people's doors, she decided to use intuition as her guide toward home. Up the road through town, then up to the right around and around, up again to the left, and then up to the right. Using the lights from homes as a guide, she made her way, her body an extraordinary mass of muscle as each heavy step through the deepened snow became, for her, a lightness, an envelopment of something more surreal than anything she had ever imagined. She clutched the violin, as if it, too, gave her strength, the momentum to reach her front door. When, at last, her next-door neighbor's door came into view, her legs, swollen with cold and exhaustion, almost collapsed under her. The reality of what she had done finally hit her. Her blue front door appeared in front of her, and she turned the handle, pushed the snow away, and heaved her body against the wood into the entryway of her home, where she fell, onto the wood, the soft dry wood of her home.

Shivering and shivering, she threw off her clothes, the soggy, frozen mass of ice still clinging to them, as she drew a bath hotter than any she had ever had. The scalding water met her skin with a sizzling sigh, her journey now over as she closed her eyes and wept.

CHAPTER THIRTEEN

Marlene took her seat on the plane. She sighed, heavy with relief. Her hands, sweating and shaking, held her ticket stub to Bucharest. She stared out the window and watched the storm pass. Thick clouds moved away as the sun began to pour through. It had rained hard that week. There were floods everywhere and life had slammed to a halt.

That week. Everything seemed to have happened that week. Over a period of seven days, her life had gone down a new path. After her meeting with the counselor, Marlene went home to think. Then she went for a long walk through the rainy streets of her city and thought some more. She repeatedly asked herself what she really wanted in life. Each time, the answer was clear: this child. She was a person who often wavered. Her flimsiness in decisions had always annoyed her. This time, however, there was not one ounce of uncertainty. Her intuition felt powerful. She did not just want to be a parent, she felt. She wanted to be *this* child's parent. Undoubtedly, she would encounter abominable circumstances, yet she sensed that she had an infinite amount of love and patience to surmount absolutely anything.

She called the counselor and said yes. The whirlwind then began. She signed papers and more papers. Each one solidified her conviction to follow this path, and each time she inscribed her name on a document, she felt closer to her own truth. The lawyer explained how the process would go: After getting the child in Romania, Marlene would become the child's legal guardian until the adoption was finalized in California. When she told her supervisor at work and all her colleagues, everyone jumped in the air and celebrated. They told her to take time off as she needed, and when she came back, they would welcome this child with open arms, no matter what her disability. When Marlene walked out the door of work that day she spoke with the lawyer, she knew that the San Francisco Bay Area, with its attitudes of acceptance and compassion, was where she wanted to raise her child.

She looked around her apartment that evening and wondered what to change, what to get rid of, and what to keep. In a week she would be a mother, and now her home was a mess. She gasped at the dust in the corners, the dirty underwear that she had not washed. Panic set in, and she cringed as she looked around her and felt overwhelmed by everything she had to do in so little time.

She slumped to the floor and experienced flashbacks of her own mother, drunk again, unable to care for anyone around her. She felt a suffocating aloneness. The tiny world she had developed, from this maimed childhood, had thick walls and contained no one except herself.

Through her closed eyes, she envisioned Thérèse. She saw her passion, her love of life, how she thrust herself into the throes of whatever came her way. In her mind, she grabbed at her, her face, her lips, and felt, as a result, a buoyancy, a flame inside that flared in all directions. When she opened her eyes, the room looked different; the plan in her head had radically altered itself. She became, at that moment, an Amazon, and as a result, she began to turn her home completely upside down. She moved furniture and hauled out of her apartment everything she did not need. She had an office, which would no longer be an office but the child's room. She emptied that room. Then she went shopping. A bed, a dresser, a rug, soft, yes, soft would be the theme. Love would enter this house, softly caressing a child who needed a home, who needed a mommy.

The day before her flight, she finished everything. She had created a home for two, for a mother and a child. There were tears, but they were silent ones, as she sat on the bed in the child's room and fingered the soft, velvety fabric.

She thought of her own mother, her last days before she succumbed to the "big dark monster," as her father had called the cancer, which took her away when Marlene was thirteen. A week before she died, her mother, consumed with pain, had her last words with her only child.

"Never have a child, Marlene," she said in the hospital in a weak, labored voice. "The day I got pregnant with you was the day my life became not my life. Your father never allowed me to have an abortion." Her body convulsed after that last statement, and the doctor had to increase the dose of morphine to help minimize the pain.

Marlene, aghast at her mother's closing statement, felt her chest tighten. For several minutes she could not breathe.

Her mother was gone just two days later. The death of her mother dug a hole in her psyche, rendering her unable to love, to not entertain even the remotest possibility of connecting with anyone on an intimate level.

Her father put her in therapy when the middle school principal told him he had to find help for his daughter, who had not said a word for months after her mother's passing.

The therapist sat with Marlene week after week in silence. Finally, one day, months after starting therapy, she spoke.

"I want to babysit," she said in a quiet voice.

"That's a lovely idea," the therapist said.

This began what would become Marlene's salvation. When she

was with young children the child inside her uncurled and was able to open her eyes. The love she had never experienced in her own childhood blossomed like a rare wildflower that the wind had transported to an empty hillside.

She graduated from middle school, high school, and then San Francisco State University with a bachelor's degree in child development. Right after her college graduation, in a freak accident, her mostly distant father died while walking his new girlfriend's dog. A car ran them over and killed them both instantly.

After the funeral, Marlene decided that the magical world of young children was her only safe place. She immediately got a job at a local childcare center, and it was there, and only there, that she thrived.

* * *

Although it was a red-eye flight, Marlene did not sleep a bit; her excitement was so huge it billowed out into the seats next to her. She could not sit still, and several times in the night, other insomniacs bumped her stray feet as they jittered in the aisle. No one was sitting in the seat next to her, which was a gift, as she could spread out all her uncontainable energy. Still, though, she needed the entire plane just to house it all. Throughout the night, flight attendants kept handing her packages of food-related items, trying to calm down this overenergized passenger. She had no appetite, though, and she pocketed all the little packages for her child.

She closed her eyes and tried to remember all the detailed instructions the counselor and the attorney had given her. The week that Marlene had been decluttering her apartment, the counselor had been on the phone, finalizing everything for her. The entire adoption process was to happen thanks to a friend of the counselor who lived in Bucharest, a well-known attorney who eventually made it her mission to release unwanted children to the homes of loving parents, wherever they came from. She told Marlene's counselor that it was her gift to San Francisco, a city that had warmly welcomed her and her lesbian partner many years earlier when she was doing her graduate work at San Francisco State University.

"As soon as you arrive in Bucharest, check in at the hotel, and make sure it is all clean and ready, so when you have the child that first night, there will be no surprises. Then, take a taxi to the orphanage. Have the taxi driver wait there for you until you are ready to leave. Check in at the front desk and tell them that Doina Cristina Moldava, or Mrs. Moldava, has organized your meeting today. They might pretend to look puzzled, and if they do, give them a hundred US dollars and they will immediately understand why you are there. Remind them that there is a file waiting for them with your name on it. Again, if they look confused, give them another one hundred dollars. In that file will be the name of the child they have arranged to be given to you.

"For reasons of confidentiality, Mrs. Moldava would not tell me anything about the identity of this child over the phone, but she insisted that she had taken to account what you requested: a girl, not older than five and not younger than two, so that she would be able to attend the day care center where you work. If, at any point, they refuse your right to this child, give them again another one hundred dollars. Please be assured that you are not abducting this child in any way, and everything has been gone over scrupulously by Mrs. Moldava. The workers at the adoption agency know this as well and might, seeing your innocent face, try to manipulate you into going back home without one of their children. Do not let them do this.

"Once they present the child to you, don't make a huge deal of showing her too much affection in front of the workers. Save that for later. It is a business deal as far as they are concerned. Do make eye contact and show warmth to the child. If she wants to show you her friends, her bed, whatever, let her. If she seems scared, that is normal. In fact, expect fear and some resistance for quite a while, for months or possibly years. Remember always that she has been severely traumatized, and even if you know you are a safe person, she won't know this. Your job is to get her out of there without a fuss and hopefully without a major tantrum. If she has one of those, which she could do, your job will be a bit more challenging but not impossible. You need to show her from the beginning, in your actions and in your facial expressions, that you are warm, capable, caring, and accepting, and that nothing daunts you. Then, take her by the hand and lead her outside to the waiting taxi, which will take you two to the hotel.

"The next day, early in the morning, you have a flight to London Heathrow, where the European Adoption Society will be waiting for you. They will manage all the remaining details before you travel back to San Francisco. The child will have a thorough medical exam, they will give her any emergency treatments needed, and they will provide a detailed report of her medicals needs to give to your doctor when you arrive back home. They will oversee all the travel documents so that there are no glitches at customs. These procedures will all be done by the end of the day, so you can catch your 10 p.m. flight to California."

As the plane flew, Marlene sat, eyes closed, near the wing of the plane, imagining the very beginnings of her motherhood, the first expression on the face of her child, her daughter. She had memorized the instructions. All that remained was to get there, to take the hand of the child, and to let love take over.

She felt it before any other passenger, the precise moment when the plane began its descent. She looked out the window to a darkened sky, much like the winter welcome Paris gave her. As roads and buildings took shape in the darkness, there were still mountains and endless miles of wilderness to greet them. The landing was rough because of turbulence from the winds that whipped around the plane. A starkness met her, grays of all shades, a jagged edge to everything. When finally, the plane landed, she sighed, an entirely different kind of sigh than the one she'd given when she entered the plane in San Francisco. This one had to it a resolve, a strength, a pulse that propelled her forward, out of her seat, out of the airport, to the awaiting taxi, her one bag in hand.

She could not see Bucharest as a tourist might, the beautiful buildings, the impressive landmarks that flitted by, the parks that went on for miles. Instead, her focus was mostly internal. In the taxi, she observed that the city seemed to speed by with an unfathomable sense of mystery. She decided that one day she would return to understand this city.

Upon arriving at the hotel, as instructed, she checked in. Then she got back in the taxi and told the driver to go to the orphanage. As they approached, the city seemed to be shuddering, everything dingy and depressed. There was not a tree or bush in sight, and the buildings that surrounded it were dilapidated, concrete structures that housed no care or concern. The orphanage itself loomed ahead with a morbid sense of urgency. The taxi parked. Marlene made sure the driver would wait for her, and she entered the mausoleum-like structure with lightness in her steps.

Everything the counselor had warned her about happened. Marlene ended up spending five hundred dollars, each time smiling inside because she knew she was on top of the game. Then the grand moment happened.

Out she came, a tiny thing, emaciated, her face gaunt and sallow. Her eyes had sunk into the folds of her skin. Her face looked ancient, softness obliterated, but she was only three years and two months old. The orphanage worker held her hand tightly, as it appeared the little girl wanted to bolt from the room. Marlene gazed into her eyes and felt her own inner tears unfold as she witnessed this event, this most precious being coming into the room. She stared at the girl, amazed at her beauty. Then, something happened that almost made Marlene drop to her knees. The child, approaching her, suddenly reached her arms up, her tiny scrawny sticks of arms, reached up toward the sky—a child's universal gesture that they want to be picked up, held, that they want to feel safe in the arms of an adult. Marlene did not know that this child had never in her short life done this before. Instinct prevailed, however, as she reached up, as Marlene took her, held her, and brought her to her chest, folding her into her softness, as together they said hello in a language that was as deep as the earth and as primitive in its expression of tenderness. The child would not let go and clung to Marlene with a grasp that was tight and determined. Marlene cooed and held her close, their cheeks rubbing against each other. From every corner of that room, there were stares. Children peeked out from the filthy edges of humanity, the ones who longed for this, gawking, their hearts swelling with the starvation that comes from their short lifetimes of wanting to be loved, wanting this, wanting this woman to be their mommy, too. For children know these things; the primitive longings call them because they are the ancestral messages of the heart. Children know what love is, and these, trapped in the confines of their already hardened world, were famished for it.

There was an unusual hush in the room as Marlene and the child clung to each other, as Marlene's strong arms held her close, as the child folded into those arms and closed her eyes. The faces of the orphanage assistants fell, for it appeared they had never seen this before. The head of the orphanage handed Marlene a file folder with one piece of paper inside. This was the child's complete file. With the folder clasped in her hand, Marlene took the child, who had fallen asleep, and slipped away into the taxi, leaving behind the dark cloisters of the building that would always be, in their minds, a somber place that had become sacred because that was where love found its calling.

CHAPTER FOURTEEN

It was 1 p.m. when Thérèse woke up to a dazzling winter sun bursting through her windows. She rubbed her eyes to awaken from the deep sleep that had been bestowed upon her and looked at the foot of the bed, where the violin lay motionless, its case a bedraggled mess. In yesterday's urgency, she had paid no attention to any of the details of the instrument or its housing. She carefully opened the latches to reveal a luscious piece of wood whose smell intoxicated her. As she picked up the instrument, she felt bathed in the immemorial, and she intuitively felt that a lifetime of ethereal music had once poured out of this instrument. She looked inside to find the date it was made, and while there was, indeed, something carved in the wood, she could not make out what it said. She held the violin to her, cradling it as if it were a child, a beautiful being that the luthier crafted out of trees most probably planted several generations earlier. She picked up the bow, tightened the hairs, and then put the violin to her chin and stroked a note. She had done this once before, played a friend's violin for five minutes, several years ago. As she stroked the instrument, as her bow arm moved up and down the A string she, even in her inexperience playing the violin, noticed something extravagantly remarkable about this piece of wood. It had a resonance to it that was infinitely sweet, a pureness of tone that spoke of an age long before her own.

She longed to phone Jakub to tell him of her discovery. She could not wait to get to Paris to have him look at the inscription inside, to listen to the sumptuousness of this violin. She realized she had missed her appointment to call him the day before, and today was Sunday, and most assuredly he would not be in his office. Still, her impatience grew, and she picked up the phone and dialed his number.

"Allô?" the voice answered.

"Ah, Jakub, it's you. How lovely. I meant to phone you yesterday, but I got stuck in the worse blizzard Grenoble has had in fifty years."

"Terrible. Did you get the violin?"

"Yes, unbelievably, I have it right in front of me. I had to walk home and abandon my car by the side of the road. But I am fine now, and this violin is a jewel, I swear to you, I think we have one of your instruments. I am off Tuesday. Can I come up and show you?" Thérèse was breathless, her excitement uncontainable.

"Absolutely! I am here all day until 6 p.m. I look forward to seeing you on Tuesday."

"Perfect, then. See you soon!"

Thérèse held the violin again. She put it up to her neck and cradled it. She imagined its owner, sixty years ago somewhere in France, in a family that celebrated the Sabbath together on a Friday evening, hands encircling the light of the candles. And then the challah and the wine would have been given, blessings on that evening as the sun dipped down. And there was love, always love around that table. She imagined someone playing that violin, ethereal sounds emanating from their home. Thérèse then imagined this family carted away, in cattle cars, to their deaths. The violin, that which had played so sweetly on the night of the Shabbat, she imagined it taken, stolen, dropped into the hands of thieves, murderers, calloused hands that knew nothing about music.

She looked out the window and watched the snow melt. She put on her thick jacket, her warmest scarf, her boots and hat, and with her car keys in her pocket and a shovel thrown against her shoulder, she began the trek to her car. With each crunch of her boots on the soft, melting powder, she recalled her journey the night before. She laughed at herself and what humans do to accomplish a mission. Children were out, laughing and sliding down the hills of the town as the sun came out.

The piece of metal that would take her home had become a white lump by the side of the road. Thérèse had to shovel for about an hour to get it to look again like her car. The road, now opened and plowed, gave her a free entrance to home, where she dried off her wet, sweaty clothes, warmed up soup and bread, and quickly went to bed and closed her eyes, as her unconscious mind dipped into a deep, dreamless sleep.

CHAPTER FIFTEEN

In the hotel room, the child slept soundly on the bed as Marlene stroked her hair, overlooking how filthy it was. To Marlene, this child was perfect in all ways, and her heart spilled over with something she could not put her finger on. She felt lost in bliss as she stared at the perfect being ensconced in her arms on the bed. She had never felt this happy.

She recalled the words she had read earlier on the single sheet of paper that contained all the information the orphanage provided. Her name was Gabriela. She was born on December 15, 1981, in the city of Bucharest. When she arrived, she was 2.6 years of age. Her height was 76.2 centimeters. Her weight was 9.98 kilos. Marlene flipped over the page, thinking that there would be more information. Her medical history? Information about her parents, any siblings, any social or emotional observations? Nothing. Marlene laughed to herself, seeing the whole picture. Here was a tiny, vastly underweight child who had most probably been dumped at that orphanage, by parents who had abandoned her, and then had somehow survived eight months of neglect and most likely abuse at the orphanage. Survival is a wonder, she mused as she stroked the soft skin of the child who clamped onto her. As she listened to Gabriela breathe heavily in her sleep, she remembered the words of the counselor, in preparing her for her departure:

"I have heard of the atrocities in these Romanian orphanages, once again, information that the public is not yet aware of. At the age of three years in these places, they give the child a test in front of a commission that has been instructed to divide the children into two groups: the 'bad' ones and the 'good' ones. The 'good' children group are the heartiest and can survive even the harshest environment. These ones are given entry into a government-sponsored educational program for children from three years to eighteen. The 'bad' ones are the weak children, usually the most sensitive ones who cannot handle shots, solitude, and other challenging childhood events. These children are given the term *handicapped*, whether it be of a psychological or physical base. Most likely, Marlene, the child that you will be given will fall under the 'bad' category, which is why they probably are more than happy to give her away. They will probably not tell you anything about the circumstances behind this determination, and you will most likely have to figure out on your own what the problem is. Hopefully, the doctors in London will assist you in finding out your child's challenges and disabilities."

Marlene gazed at her daughter; her eyes soft as she listened to the regular rhythm of her breath. There had been no words spoken yet between the two of them, but in their gestures, there was a bond, an insistence on touch. She noticed how the child had focused in on her face, studying it. She had made no sounds, only grunts, and she knew that for most children of her age language development was one of the major milestones. While she was intent on this study, this silent inspection of Gabriela, an expressiveness in her face, a desire to know more, became clear. When the taxi driver had said a few words to her in Romanian, her face had looked blank, distant. Marlene, in her rudimentary knowledge of the language, understood that he had called her beautiful and he had said something that appeared to be a joke, but the child did not respond. Marlene was not sure if Gabriela hadn't heard him or if she was just being cautious with someone she didn't know.

"Gabriela," Marlene said aloud, quietly repeating her name. It was beautiful, she thought; she loved the way it rolled off the tongue like a song. Perhaps she is Deaf. Perhaps anything. Diagnoses and developmental expectations of young children, which she had become an expert on, meant, at that moment, nothing to her. In all her experience with attachment and bonding with three-year-old children, what she and Gabriela had, from that first moment, was all that mattered. She felt an elated rush just knowing her daughter gripped her hand in her sleep. The rush turned to a gentle lulling. It was love, she decided, as she moved closer to the child, to her Gabriela, and as her arms firmly wrapped themselves around this tiny thing, she too fell into a deep and relaxed sleep.

CHAPTER SIXTEEN

"*Mon Dieu!*" Jakub exclaimed when his assistant had scoped the violin and had examined each crevice, especially the interior. Thérèse looked at their faces and then down at the violin that glistened under the bright lights.

Almost obscured, and only visible with the special scoping and the super-bright lights, was the simple word *Guarneri 1738*.

Then, deeply hidden in the back folds of the wood, inside, next to the sound post, was a Star of David.

"The family heirloom," Thérèse stated. All three had tears in their eyes.

Philippe, the assistant, a luthier, and specialist in early violins, took off his gloves, held the instrument, and cradled it to his neck. He took the bow, also from the eighteenth century, ivory lacing the frog or end part, and tightened it.

"May I?" he asked, rhetorically.

"YES. Please," she replied.

He began to play Bach's *Partita for Violin No. 2*, staying mostly on the D and G strings. Occasionally he went up to the higher notes, creating a resonance that plunged into the heart, a sense of timelessness. The Guarneri graced each note with a feeling of the angelic, a sweetness that blended with its age, a sensuous quality nothing could surpass. When Philippe finished, there was silence that lasted several minutes, as the three of them stood, amazed

62

at the brilliance of this instrument and the fact that it had been found. The echo of the last notes resounded within them.

Jakub quietly said, "I know the owner. He was my father's best friend."

Thérèse and Phillippe gulped.

"When I was a young child, I went to his home often with my parents. After dinner, he played for us. This violin has the exact same sound. I know this was his violin."

He began to cry then, huge sobs that puddled down by his feet.

"I see them," he blurted out, sobbing. "My parents, those nights by the fire, listening to what I thought was the most beautiful sound coming out of my father's friend's violin. For years, way after my parents were murdered and I, the only survivor, remained to find some semblance of humanity, for years, the sounds of that violin resonated in my brain, giving me a reason to live. I often wondered what had happened to that violin, the object that had become for me greater than life."

Phillippe handed the violin to Jakub. He put it up to his nose and inhaled, and then kissed the wood. His tears streamed down and wet the fingerboard. He looked up at the sky and thanked the universe, and then he cradled the instrument as if it were his own child, a masterpiece, a work of genius, an emblem of the transcendence of humankind.

"Is there family that survived?" Thérèse asked.

He nodded. "A son. Living in America with his wife and two children."

A profound silence filled the room as he went to the phone, looked at a piece of paper on his desk, got the number, and dialed.

A male voice answered. "Hello?"

"Hello, is this Mr. Lieberman?"

"Yes."

"This is Jakub Bernovitch from the Association of Looted Music in Paris. I have your father's violin."

There was silence on the other end of the phone.

Then there was a scream. "Oh my God! Tell me! Ruth, come to the phone, they found Papa's violin!"

A woman's scream, high pitched and echoing, followed, as footsteps could be heard. His wife ran to the phone.

"Are you sure?"

"Yes, Oskar, as sure as I know my name. I recognized the sound even before I looked inside with my specialist here and read the label, gazed at the Star of David next to the sound post." His voice trailed off a bit. "I remember so fondly all those nights your father played that violin." He began to cry again, hearing the sobs on the other end of the phone, two men who had miraculously survived the atrocities of the camps, grieving all those in their families who had not. Two men who had grown up and had somehow resumed their lives.

Jakub pressed his ear to the phone, as the son of his father's best friend continued to cry, as his wife next to him wailed too, all the way from America, the crackling phone lines connecting them.

"Can you do something for me?" Oskar said through his tears.

"Of course. Anything."

"Can you, or someone there play something, anything, on that violin?"

"Absolutely."

Jakub nodded to Philippe and whispered, "Can you play something for Mr. Lieberman?"

Philippe nodded and picked up the violin. He put a silken cloth under his chin and grabbed the bow.

As Jakub held the phone up in the air, Philippe caressed the Guarneri like a treasured child. He effortlessly moved his fingers up and down the fingerboard in sync with the bow, producing sounds that echoed in that room and through the phone, from

Paris to Chicago, a piece by Paganini.

"My father played that piece," was all they heard, several minutes after Philippe was done.

"I will book a flight to Paris for early next week," Oskar said. Tears overcame him again, as he mumbled something.

His wife began to speak, her own voice shaky and vulnerable. "How can we thank you, Jakub?"

"You have my assistant to thank, Mrs. Lieberman. She found the violin in Grenoble, in a thrift shop, in the middle of a snowstorm."

"Please call me Ruth. And I need to meet your assistant. We owe everything to her, and to you."

"Your family's violin is what matters. Lives come and lives go; some irretrievably are stolen away, but underneath, there is a piece of wood in my hands, which will soon be in yours, that transcends all the ugliness of humankind and moves us all to places of tears. That, for me, is life."

"Mazel tov." Jakub could hear tears through those words.

"And to you and to your family as well."

"See you next week."

"Absolutely."

Each person held the phone, now disconnected, as witnesses stood by in Paris and in Chicago. There was a hush on each continent, a sigh, as winter flailed outside, reminding each one of the harshness of life. Meanwhile, the violin glowed from within as if it had its own spirit, wood encased in hope, in the ascendance of all that was, to a future that would now hold music, beautiful music made from trees that lived centuries ago and hands that would create sensational sounds, from father to son and onward.

CHAPTER SEVENTEEN

A few hours later, Marlene woke up to her daughter wailing. Her hands were soaked, and her entire body was covered in sweat. Her cries became primal grunts, loud and insistent. Marlene looked at Gabriela's anguished face and knew she must be starving. She had refused any food since they had met hours earlier. According to the clock, it was 9 p.m. for the child and the middle of the night for her. Urine covered her daughter's clothes, and all the sheets were drenched. She got on the phone and called for room service, but no one spoke English. She remembered, then, her quick tutorial from the adoption advisor.

"*Ajutor! E o urgenta!*" she cried into the phone.

The receptionist rattled away, and Marlene had not the foggiest idea what she was saying. Gabriela's wails became louder, and she figured that the receptionist would hear them in the background and do something. Gabriela began to thrash on the soaked bed and refused to let Marlene touch her, even though her expression was pleading. Marlene stared at her distressed daughter's face with a calm, reassuring look.

Then there was a knock on the door.

Marlene opened it, relieved. Somehow, they knew, the hotel people. They remembered her checking in, the American with the little child. In the woman's cart was a change of sheets and dinner. Marlene reached over to hug the bulbous woman as she took in the child's distressed. She went to Gabriela and rattled off something in her mother tongue, but the screaming prevailed. Then she handed Marlene a glass of milk. Marlene stroked her daughter's hair as she handed her the plastic glass and watched as she gulped down the smooth white liquid. There was a hush in the room, the cacophony silenced as she drank the nourishing substance. When she was done, the hotel maid handed her a sandwich, and the smell of fresh bread wafted through the room. Gabriela tore at the bread, inhaling the soft flavors of yeast. The contents of the sandwich spilled out all over the bed, but she plucked them from the wet sheets and devoured each bite. She shoved huge gulps of food into her mouth. It appeared that she hadn't eaten in months. Looking at her tiny frame, Marlene wondered if she had ever eaten like this.

The hotel maid made a gesture toward her nose, indicating that the smell was a bit strong. She went over to her cart and pointed at the clean sheets. Marlene went to her bag and pulled out some clean clothes. The maid went into the bathroom, and as Marlene held her daughter, the maid cleaned her body with a warm, wet washcloth. She took the soiled clothes and put them in her dirty laundry bag. Without words, there was a quiet, gentle rhythm to it all. The child closed her eyes, a contented expression on her face, as Marlene held her close and breathed in her now sweet smells. When she finished putting clean sheets on the bed, she laid Gabriela back down and pulled the covers over her minuscule frame. She paid the maid a generous sum and then returned to the bed and held her daughter, watching the rhythmic sounds of her breath as she fell back asleep. Marlene saw that the maid had left an extra sandwich for her and realized that she, too, was famished. She tore at the sandwich as her daughter had, just minutes earlier, chuckling to herself as the taste of the chicken blended with the softness of the bread, and the food tamed her belly as she fell back into a deep, replenishing sleep.

* * *

Light blazoned through the windows, a crisp winter sun that enveloped Marlene and Gabriela, waking them both, announcing to the world that a new day had risen. There was a small knock on the door, and Marlene, wrapped around her daughter, pulled herself away as Gabriela's eyes followed her movements. On the other side of the door, a tray lay on the floor, with a glass of milk and a cup of coffee, rolls, jams, and butter. She smiled. Tears welled up in her eyes that she brushed away as she brought over the tray to the bed. Gabriela was sitting up, smiling, her face radiant.

She gulped down the milk as Marlene sipped the hot coffee, each one savoring the tastes of the morning. Marlene helped her daughter spread fresh butter and jam on the rolls, and watched the child devour the food, jam spreading over her face like makeup. She laughed and took a napkin and wiped her daughter's face when she finished, and every single crumb had been eaten.

Gabriela got off the bed then and headed to the bathroom, and after she peed, she stared at the shower and pointed to it. Marlene gestured and pointed at the water faucet, and then at their clothes that they needed to take off. Gabriela nodded, and quickly they both removed their night clothes. When the water was hot enough, Gabriela took Marlene's hand and led her inside the shower. She held onto Marlene's leg as the hot water cascaded down her tiny body. Marlene took the washcloth and gently soaped her daughter's small frame. Then she washed her hair that probably hadn't been washed in weeks. They stayed there under the cascading stream for a long time, letting the water sluice over their bodies until it started to cool. Marlene turned off the tap. She grabbed the towels, wrapped them around the child, and held her close as she dried off her hair and her body, and then her own. She stepped back to witness a glimmer in her daughter's face, as if she knew that she was beginning something huge in her little life.

Moments later, dressed, they were out the door, hand in hand, a statuesque woman who spoke only English and a minuscule amount of Romanian, and a minuscule child who would never know an auditory language. From a distance the two fit, somehow, as if they were two stray puzzle pieces whose search was finally over, feeling a sense of completion in finding each other. Marlene hailed a taxi to the airport. In her bag were two tickets to London Heathrow. While each of their faces looked serious and focused on the present, there was a subtle expression, one that hinted at the significance of this moment in each of their lives. As their hands clasped, one big hand to one tiny one, they became united in effecting this transformation, their lives altered, their worlds changed.

* * *

She did not know what a mother was, as she had never known language, and memories of her birth mother had disappeared. But as she clasped the hand of the woman next to her, this large woman with big hands, something inside her stirred, something she had never experienced before in her few years on this planet. She felt rocked, swayed to some internal music, some force that screamed out, but gently. She needed this, she wanted this, her life depended on this, this woman. There were strong feelings in her that she had no name for. Had she had spoken language, she would have said "Mama," but without the ability to hear or speak, she had no label for Marlene.

And because there was no language that she could understand coming from the mouth of this woman who held her hand so tightly, as they slipped into a white car that zipped through the streets of the busy city, she did not know where she was going. She had no idea that they were to go on one of those things that fly in the air, that they would end up in England, and then shortly after, that they would take a much bigger plane on a much longer trip to a place very far away. Somehow, she knew, in her tiny self, that this adventure was just beginning. She felt something like tears inside her, but they did not fall. Her heart was being pushed open, and something beautiful was there. What some instinctive force inside her commanded was to hold tight onto that hand, the huge, soft hand of this woman who made her rock and sway inside, who led her from one step to another, from one phase of life to the next.

CHAPTER EIGHTEEN

From the train, Thérèse stared at France whizzing by. She felt empty without the violin by her side. She recognized that from this first find, she had begun to form a new relationship with herself and the outside world. She experienced a sense of wholeness that came from finding something that would bring together a family. She had never been able to gather her own family, never could resolve the mental instability of her own mother, after whose death she felt a pain in her own heart that would pierce her daily like a freshly sharpened knife.

She replayed in her head the whole episode in Paris, the conversations of the family in America, the sighs, the joy, the relief, the love. It was love, she said to herself, that had survived the atrocities that had besieged this family, and in the violin, the carved ancient wood, love had been transmitted from one being to another. She smiled to herself, a wide smile that lit up her face. The light poured from the outside world downward, across her roughened cheekbones and illuminated a moment in time where love resonated within her very being. It was survival, after all—survival not in some heroic sense, but more a need to connect, to rejuvenate, to allow a family to continue its path with meaning.

That's what this work is about, finding these instruments, uncovering a love so strong it can never be conquered. I will continue this search, this search for instruments, wherever it takes me.

71

With that resolution firmly embedded in her consciousness, she closed her eyes and let the landscape drift silently by. The rolled bales of hay melded into the green of the grass that pushed itself from the ground—life perpetuating life. As sleep permeated her exhausted being, her own inner landscape took its own form of a life uncovered. Her breathing became slow and heavy as the rhythm of the train lulled her into a dream:

Her hair blew in the wind; the gentle folds of dark strands covered her face. She was holding something in her arms, no, there was something in each arm: in one, there was something bundled in a blanket, a child, a baby perhaps, asleep, covered and protected; and in the other, there was a violin, a curved piece of wood that had not yet been varnished, the unfinished instrument held dearly in her left hand. The woman gazed out at an ocean, the vast expanse of water cradling her thoughts as she held the two beings in her hands, her face sublime, as if she was holding all her life's dreams in those two hands. The wind continued to swirl around her face, her expression of contentment unwavering.

The train conductor jolted Thérèse awake. They had arrived in Grenoble. She quickly gathered her coat, her purse, and descended the train, still in a fog, half asleep, still in the space of her dream.

As the cold seeped into her tired self, Thérèse trudged to her car in the parking lot. She started the engine, turning on the heat full blast until she was ready to leave. Once on the highway, heading out of town, her mind again began to roam and focused on the dream, and on Marlene who seemed to be the woman in the dream. *Again, she surfaces. Why now? Always in these pivotal moments, she comes to my mind, my dreams, as if she is a talisman reflecting a path in my life. The baby…the violin…* She imagined what it would be like to have this woman's hair brushing against her face in the wind. *Cradling* was the word that came to her, the children attended to and loved, the violin, the ocean itself, the forces of nature that brought them all together.

As she drove, Thérèse felt a momentary longing to reach out, to touch her hand, to stroke the lips of this woman who continued to return to her thoughts when she least expected it. A warm glow consumed Thérèse as she headed toward home, the familiar road that led off the highway, up and around, past the little village, traversing open fields, small farmhouses, until she arrived at the roughness and comfort of her front door.

Once inside the threshold, that moment when there is the familiar sigh upon reaching home, she went straight to her bed, and without even taking a stitch of clothing off except her shoes, she collapsed into the soft duvet and let the world of sleep surround her, seeping into the crevices of all that she had experienced that day.

CHAPTER NINETEEN

The whirr of Bucharest's Aurel Vlaicu International Airport jostled their senses. Sounds and smells and the cacophony of a frenzied life spewed out in front of them. Marlene looked at the clock on the boarding signs. Despite her limited knowledge of the language, she realized they were late, and the boarding gates would close in ten minutes. The airport monitor indicated that it would take eleven minutes to get to their destination to board the plane. She picked up Gabriela and began to run. Adrenaline filled her jet-lagged and exhausted self and boomeranged through her body, as her brand-new child bobbed up and down in her arms, her eyes wide open to all that was happening.

With thirty seconds to spare, Marlene presented her tickets at the desk, as the harried attendant gave her a consternated look, tore her tickets, returned the stub, and then closed the gates behind her. Still holding Gabriela, she plopped into her seat, her breath labored as sweat ran down from her armpits onto her belly and under her breasts. A flight attendant spoke quickly in Romanian and pointed at her unfastened seatbelt. Gabriela looked around her, at the people next to her, and then, after Marlene had strapped her in, she stared out the window, at the wings of the plane that stuck out, ready to take flight. She grabbed onto her mother's hand, which was still sweaty, and clutched it tightly. Marlene, taking a deep breath, squeezed it back and let her relief spill out through all her pores.

In the space of less than two days I feel so united with this tiny child. This union is all-consuming. She smiled, loving it.

As her child stared out the window, her gaze fixed on the wings, Marlene still held Gabriela's little hand. Each step of this journey was monumental. She felt it, and she could sense that Gabriela could feel it too. As she looked at the child who seemed giddy with delight, Marlene felt her own giddiness, her own experience of a primal connection, a connection to something inside her that symbiotically bonded with another human being. All at once the painting by Berthe Morisot came into her mind, the angelic look the mother directed toward her child, and as the plane began to taxi away from the boarding gate, as it maneuvered toward the waiting line of ascending planes, as it eventually took off into the murky skies of Bucharest, a slow, and then a quick ascent into and then past the clouds, Marlene began to cry. Her tears blended with her smiles, and the moisture dropped onto the hand of her tiny child. Gabriela turned to her mother and saw the tears, and took her hand and wiped them, as she put her other hand around Marlene's arm and held it there. Marlene smiled and felt this little hand stuck to her arm with a kind of adhesive between them that would never allow them to be parted.

Gabriela turned back to the window, fixed on the wings, as Marlene closed her eyes and found contentment in that moment of peace in which she knew she was exactly where she should be. Floating in her consciousness was the image of Thérèse, an amorphous shape that lacked detail. Although the picture was fuzzy, she was holding something in her hands, and on her face was a smile, a warm expression of joy, of invitation, of comfort. Marlene smiled at this image and felt a warm glow inside her that left her with the sensation of melting, melding herself into the folds of this other woman's existence. There was a permanence to it all, this recurring image of Thérèse. As Marlene dozed off, she remembered that her colleague and friend Juanita told her once to never forget that life is beautiful. This voice resounded in her like a poem as sleep arrived and took her to another place. Gabriela's eyes grew heavy and closed, as sleep took her away. Her hand dug gently into the soft folds of her now sleeping mother.

CHAPTER TWENTY

Thérèse's life as a psychiatrist was as bone-chilling as it was sublime. There were moments when she had to take deep breaths while listening to the harrowing stories of her clients. Hers was not a colorless profession, and each morning, from her early days as an intern working her way through school to the present, as she sauntered into her office, coffee cup in hand, she never knew what stories she would hear that day. A client once told her that she fit perfectly in her profession, that she had found her calling listening to others, being a rock in people's lives. Thérèse was taken aback by this nonchalant comment from this client who had worked with her for upwards of ten years, every week diligently spilling out the horrors that had framed her life. When this client decided to terminate her work with Thérèse, there was a sense of awe in the room, a feeling of wonder at how this had happened, this healing, this arduous weekly work that produced such a favorable outcome, such a wholeness in that client's approach to life now. It was as if a curtain made of cement had been smashed open and left only a fine linen fabric, flowing in the breeze. She remembered vividly that last day when both client and therapist were crying, that sense of completion finally hitting, the sublime of the healing meeting and chasing away the ghastly horrors of a life untended.

For all the years she had done this work, this listening, she had begun to realize that indeed she had a calling, something that went beyond career choice. She knew that her mother's mental illness had become embedded in her psyche. There were times when a client presented a similar scenario from his or her own past. When this happened, Thérèse wept inside for her own loss, memories of her mother's suicide tormenting her. In the psychology world, when a client's words or behaviors elicit a personal, often unconscious response in the therapist, it is called "countertransference." Beyond the technical term, Thérèse found in herself a resonance with her clients, a kind of pain, a primitive angst. Without saying a word to her clients of her own past, Thérèse found her calling by simply listening, by guiding each client toward their own healing from whatever had held them captive.

At the end of each day, when she slipped into her Citroën, started up the engine, and headed out of Grenoble toward the highway, she heaved a habitual sigh of relief that the day was over, knowing that it had been a satisfying day but nonetheless one that exhausted her. She often wondered what it might be like to be a dancer, onstage after the performance was over, applause coming from every angle, flowers thrown onto the stage, and still more flowers in the dressing room. Pain was an insidious thing, people's pain, so vast it felt like she crossed hemispheres every day at her job. When she finally could sigh in her car and begin her journey home, she would also turn on the radio. She adored the speakers in her car, which had beautiful sound quality. The notes of a symphony would serenade her, each nuance striking, its flow around her car coming to her ears, her finely tuned ears that held each note as if they were gifts presented to her on a birthday.

Thérèse walked inside her cottage and ceremoniously threw off her hat, gloves, and thick scarf. She loved the smell of her home. She unbuttoned her jacket and walked over to her phone, where a light was blinking. Someone had left her a message.

"Good evening, Madame. I just received word that a Monsieur Havre,

the owner of a shop in Lausanne, has recently acquired a cello that would demand our immediate attention. Are you able to get out there in the next twenty-four hours? If so, it would require a bit of money, of course, in cash. The name of the shop is 'Havre etc.' They are open until 17h 30 on Fridays. The address is 44, rue des Petites Roses. Please phone me as soon as you get this message. In the meantime, I will let them know you will be there."

Giddiness filled Thérèse's mind. *Another quest for an instrument. The treasure hunt continues,* she said to herself as she replayed the message, loving the urgency of this quest, the urgency behind finding these instruments. Tomorrow was Friday. She worked a half day, and then she would be free to take the train to Lausanne. She rummaged through her pile of train schedules, finding the Grenoble-Lausanne pamphlet at the very bottom. There was a train that left at 11 a.m. and one that left at 2 p.m. It was a three-hour journey. She had a client from 11 a.m. to noon, so she would have to take the 2 p.m., cutting it close: after the taxi ride from the station to the shop, she would just make the deadline. She had a sense of déjà vu, remembering how she barely got to the shop in Grenoble the last time.

That night, sleep evaded her completely; her only thoughts were of the cello. Her excitement had increased after she phoned Jakub. He'd told her that a middle-aged, frumpy-looking *hausfrau* had brought the cello in just that morning. She told the shop owner that her son refused to practice, and it took up too much room in their small house.

"It's the ones who know nothing of music, nothing of the value and beauty of the instrument, those are the ones whose instruments we are seeking," he reminded Thérèse. "Those instruments are often the stolen ones that have somehow been placed in ignorant hands."

As she lay restless in bed, Thérèse mulled over his last line. To be ignorant of music, to have acquired somehow those stolen jewels, and to know nothing of the beauty that lay within. She did not know which crime was worse: to have in one's possession another family's heirloom, or to own an instrument with no knowledge of how to play it. *When musical instruments become commodities, the brilliance of them gets lost. Isn't it enough that these instruments are stolen?* For each of these mysterious finds, she realized, the salt on the wound grows knowing that this instrument was left aside, played by roughened, calloused, and naive hands, thrown in dusty corners, abandoned to ears that knew nothing of music.

At 2 p.m. the next day, ticket in hand, Thérèse sat in her seat in the train and watched Grenoble quietly disappear. As the sturdy piece of metal maneuvered its way through the mountains, heading towards Chambéry, the last stop in France, she smiled. She loved the mountains, the vastness that surrounded her, the majestic peaks of the Alps that never ceased to elevate her spirit. She was sleepy, exhausted, but her eyes refused to close because she wanted to continue to observe her surroundings. As the train ambled through mountain tunnels, its massive weight charting a path into Switzerland, she imagined the cello that she was about to touch, her fingers on that fingerboard, the bow in her other hand. She imagined herself leaning into the instrument as if it were her lover, feeling the wood enter her soul as she created beauty, music that resounded and echoed off the peaks of the Alps.

* * *

The trip into Lausanne was a sumptuous display of mountainous peaks. At a mere 1,726 feet, the majestic, busy city greeted her, just as her eyes were beginning to shut, preparing for an extended nap. Her stop, the end of the line, brought the train to a gentle refrain, whereupon she quickly hurled herself out of her seat and onto the platform. She hailed a taxi. Friday afternoon rush hour barraged the car, and an otherwise five-minute trip took twenty-five minutes.

At 5:25pm, Thérèse arrived at 44, rue des Petites Roses and rapped on the door of a shop that bore a handwritten sign.

"Unexpected early closure today of shop due to family emergency. Will reopen in one week."

Thérèse felt tears well up in her eyes. She had clear memories of the shop in Grenoble on that freezing day as the snow blew its incessant layers of white around her.

She knocked harder. And then knocked even harder. All she heard was her own troubled sighs, and all she felt was the ache in her knuckles.

A woman walked by and stared at Thérèse and her incessant stubbornness at the door.

"His wife is having a baby. He had to leave early, as she went into labor sooner than expected," she murmured, not to inform but seemingly to chastise the insensitivity of this strange woman who wouldn't stop pounding on a door that could cave in at any moment.

"Thank you, Madame. Do you please have any idea which hospital she might be in? I am a relative, and I came here from far away to look after her once the baby is born."

The woman stared at her incredulously. She didn't seem to believe this story. "You are from France," she mumbled, under her breath. "Always the French are so impetuous. Hôpital des Vierges Bénies," she said, walking on. Her face reflected disdain and hostility.

Thérèse walked to the main road and hailed a taxi, and within thirty minutes she was at the Hospital of the Blessed Virgins.

She repeated the story to the hospital attendant and told the young blonde woman that she was Madame Havre's close cousin, and she would like to wait with Monsieur Havre until the baby was born, that Madame Havre had personally asked her to be present at the birth of her child.

"Oui, Madame, of course," she responded in a sweet, tiny voice. "They are in the birthing wing, ninth floor."

"Merci," Thérèse smiled, and as she got into the elevator, it was there, alone, that she cursed out loud, wondering what to do with her ridiculous lie.

As she exited the elevator, the ninth floor greeted her with voluminous screams from rooms where infants were coming steadfastly into the world at large.

She easily found the front desk, where an array of women seemed unexpectedly calm in a wing where drama unfolded itself around the clock.

"Excuse me, Madame? I am looking for the room of Madame Havre."

"You are?"

"Her cousin. I am also a midwife. Madame Havre asked me to be present at the birth, and since she went into early labor, I was not able to get here sooner. I just finished attending the birth of a client in Chambéry."

"That's interesting. Madame Havre did not mention that a midwife was called to the delivery."

Thérèse was sweating as the story in her mind unfolded so easily. Never in her life had she ever lied like this. The receptionist paged the head nurse, and a round woman in baby-pink scrubs pranced to the front desk.

"Your name, please?" she stated with authority.

"Thérèse, Thérèse Le Duc."

"Madame Le Duc, there is a complication here in the birth. The umbilical cord is tightly wrapped around the neck, and you came at the right time. Please quickly get into these scrubs and meet me in room nine."

Thérèse went into the changing room in the back of the wing, and as she quickly threw off her clothes and put on the blue scrubs, she felt her heart beating irregularly, her breathing erratic. Her face was bright red.

She remembered then how a client of hers, years ago, an obstetrician described this exact same process. *Think, girl, think*, she muttered to herself. *Remember exactly what he told you he did.*

As Thérèse stumbled through the hallway to room nine, loud, incessant screams surrounded her as she was whisked in by the nurses.

"Where is Monsieur Havre?" Thérèse asked innocently, donning her gloves.

"Fast asleep, slumped in the chair in the waiting room," announced one of the nurses.

This prompted the entire birthing crew to laugh. A perfect entrance for Thérèse.

"So, it's a case of a nuchal cord, where the umbilical cord is tightly wrapped around the neck?" she asked, proud that she had remembered the correct terminology.

"Yes," the head nurse responded.

"Have we checked the baby's heart rate? Any issues with blood flow?"

"All normal."

Thérèse realized in that moment that all eyes were turned to her. The doctor had had to step out of the room, as a mother in the room down the hall was going into cardiac arrest, and he had to bolt down the corridor as the code blue alarm sounded.

Sweat poured down her entire frame, and she was starting to give off a very unpleasant odor.

"Have her keep pushing. As soon as the head is out, we will clamp and cut the cord before the shoulders emerge. Let me see, though, if I can loosen the cord."

Thérèse lathered her glove with lubricant, plunged her hand into Madame Havre's womb and felt a hardened mass. Adrenaline soared through her body as she felt life, a head, a tiny being folded up tightly, a new life waiting to emerge. Everything became suspended in the room in that moment, as Thérèse found the umbilical cord, indeed wrapped tight as a rubber band around the neck. Without thinking, she whispered something into the vaginal opening, a prayer to unleash what was blocking the path toward birth. Her fingers were unusually deft, like the fingers of a musician, the fingers she never had all her life, as she handled the cord, finding its slippery contours wrap around her own hand like a silken thread. Without having had a single course, without ever having put her hand on an almost newborn baby, she instinctively loosened the nuchal cord, unwinding it like a snake, letting it free to be that passage from the child to the mother. As she gracefully pulled out her hand, like a dancer beautifully executing a performance, she quietly said, with insistence in her voice, "PUSH, with all your might, here it is. Just one more push."

Thérèse put her hand on the mother's belly as Madame Havre grunted and screamed and grunted and screamed, and as everyone was sweating in that room, as the primitive smells of women enveloped that sacred space, out came a tiny child, a girl, who immediately latched onto the bosom of her mother, who panted still, who smiled, who sighed with relief.

The nurse went out of the room to wake up the father. He opened his eyes and bolted to his wife. He picked up his new daughter as everyone beamed. Thérèse stood at the corner of the room, smiling, wondering how she got in this place.

"We have your wife's cousin Thérèse to thank for the survival of your daughter. The doctor had an emergency to deal with, and your cousin's expert midwifery rescued this child, who might not have made it otherwise," the head nurse sang out.

"My wife's cousin Thérèse? She doesn't have a cousin by that name. And no one in the family has any ties to midwifery, none that I know of at least." He held his daughter and cooed at her neck while his wife lay sleeping.

Everyone in the room looked over at Thérèse, who wanted to hide under the hospital bed.

"He's right. I am not his cousin. I came for the cello," she blurted out, needing, after all this time, for the truth to come out.

"The cello?" Monsieur Havre looked with astonishment at Thérèse.

"Yes, Monsieur. You spoke with Monsieur Bernovitch the other day, the specialist in Paris. He told you I was to come down late this afternoon to purchase the cello that had just come in. I arrived moments too late and saw a sign on the door that you would be gone for the week. I knew I couldn't wait. Many people are waiting for me."

Monsieur Havre continued to look at Thérèse inquisitively. "But how did you know to come here?"

"Your neighbor told me where you were. I lied and told her I was the cousin."

"Well, well," he sang out. "No matter all that. We needed a midwife, obviously, and you came just at the right time."

"I am not a midwife," she blurted out again. Her face turned bright red. She so wanted to hide under that bed, or even better, to run out of that hospital.

Madame Havre woke up, looking quite startled.

"You're not?" the head nurse asked.

"No." Thérèse's face looked as sheepish as they come.

"But how did you know how to deliver my baby?" Monsieur Havre asked.

Thérèse shrugged her shoulders. "I guess being a woman makes you know these things."

Everyone was quiet then.

Madame Havre spoke. "Well, she saved our baby. Get her the

cello, Antoine, and let her go home. She must be exhausted. And so am I."

"We shall name our daughter Thérèse, what do you think, Mathilde?

Madame Havre looked lovingly at her husband. "Absolutely."

* * *

Thérèse sat on the train to Paris. In the dark of night, the train rumbled through magnitudinous alpine peaks. The slow screech of the wheels created a hum in Thérèse's ears as one hand lay on her chest and the other on the cello next to her. Fast asleep with a smile on her face, she murmured something unintelligible while in her dreams, babies were everywhere, held in mothers' arms, finding peace there.

CHAPTER TWENTY-ONE

"Your child is profoundly Deaf, with a 99.8 percent hearing loss in the right year and a 99.9 percent loss in the left ear. She has what is called permanent sensorineural deafness, caused by severe damage to the inner ear, specifically a cochlear malfunctioning. Although we can't know for certain the cause of it, my guess is that her mother had rubella during pregnancy and the disease was passed down to the fetus. We see this often with children from underdeveloped countries where the rubella vaccination is not readily available. The Deafness is permanent, and her loss is so significant, even surgery for a cochlear implant would most likely be ineffective."

The doctor looked straight into Marlene's eyes.

"But the good news is that she is as healthy as a horse. She checked out fine in all our tests for the heart, lungs, and gastro-intestinal functioning. She is negative for head lice and skin diseases, and she manifests no other contagious diseases. She's much smaller than what is typical for her age, so it's likely that she was born prematurely. We often see this with adoptive children, but it is often the case that a child can mature to a normal body size and weight with a healthy and balanced diet and adequate exercise. We will need to give her vaccinations before you leave the UK, as she has had none, according to our records. She will not be able to be admitted to the US without them. So momentarily, the nurse will come in and do those. You are to follow up with your doctor in California within two weeks of your arrival to complete the vaccinations."

Marlene looked over at Gabriela, who was playing contentedly in a corner with some blocks. She was making a tower and smiling to herself.

"You have a lovely child there. She has a very pleasant demeanor. She has obviously been through a lot, but survival seems to be her middle name." The doctor smiled. "Do you have any questions?" He looked at Marlene with warmth in his eyes.

"I don't think so. I mean, probably I should. I will probably think of loads of questions once I leave. I am just so happy she is healthy. The Deafness, yes, that will be her odyssey her entire life, but I will accompany her and make sure she is not on that journey alone. There is an excellent School for the Deaf across the bay from where I live, in Berkeley. And I fortunately live in a part of the world where it is relatively easy to access disabled services."

"Learning sign language might be one of the first steps you take, for her and for you."

"I was just thinking this myself. You read my mind. I am a preschool teacher, and the plan is that during her preschool years she will be with me at the school where I work. I would like to turn the school into a sign language immersion school, where everyone will learn the language, so that we can attract other young children from the San Francisco Bay Area. I know my colleagues will be on board with this."

"Fabulous idea." They both looked over at Gabriela, who appeared immersed in her world of characters. Now, she took little figures—a mom and a child, a girl—and had them pretend to be in a home. They were apparently inseparable. She had the mom take the girl everywhere, around the house, up and down the buildings she had made, and in the house that she had also put together with blocks. The child was continually attached to the mother.

"She spells it all out right there, doesn't she?"

"She does," Marlene nodded. "Thank you so much for your gentle and thorough evaluation of her," she added.

"My pleasure. You have a got a jewel of a girl there." The doctor extended his hand, shook Marlene's, and was out the door.

His receding footsteps echoed down the hallway. Soon after, a round, short woman in white entered the room.

Gabriela looked up. Fear emanated from her face.

"Hello, lovey," the woman chirped in a I'm-trying-to-be-friendly voice. On her face was plastered a worn, fake smile.

"I'll need to do some injections," she said, looking at Marlene. "Can you please have her sit up on the table? I can't do them when she is on the floor."

Marlene stooped down and put her hand on Gabriela's back and stroked it. She motioned to the table. Gabriela looked at the nurse in white. Her face seethed. A guttural sound emanated from her tiny frame. She started to scream, then howl.

"Does this happen often?" Marlene asked the nurse.

Without saying a word, the nurse headed out of the room and down the corridor. Her footsteps pounded the linoleum floor. Gabriela returned to her play and became absorbed once again. This time, she brought in a new character, a stout woman, and the little girl hit her and banged her against the wall.

A few minutes later, a tiny woman dressed in cowboy boots entered the room. Gabriela looked over and stared at the boots. She stared at the heels and the ribbing of the leather. The woman knelt and quietly watched Gabriela's play and smiled, sweetly. Her face looked like a bird's, soft and feathery, and her frizzy blonde hair stuck out in all directions, as if it was ready to take flight. The light in the room flickered off her hair, giving the young woman a glow. Gabriela moved her eyes from the boots to her hair and stared at it, too. She put out her hand and fingered the woman's hair as they both giggled. The woman took her hand and held it for a minute, as Gabriela stared in her eyes.

The nurse in white then quietly reentered the room with a syringe in her hand. She knelt on the other side of Gabriela and, without even a blink, quickly swabbed her arm with antiseptic. Gabriela turned her head and screamed again, dropped the hand of the woman in boots, and scampered farther under the table, making her body into a tightened ball.

With a gentleness in her face that never once wavered, the woman in boots with the birdlike hair quietly took all the little play people and put them in a semicircle around Gabriela. The two of them sat across from each other under the table. Gabriela looked into the eyes of the kind young woman, and then she perused the little assemblage of people. She picked up the woman that earlier had been designated as the mother and had her sit next to the little girl. Gabriela pretended there was something in the mother's hand, and she took that pretend thing and stabbed it into the child's right arm. Gabriela made a face, a pained face, and the pretend girl sat quietly, and then the mother took the thing out, and then they went back to the attaching behaviors that Gabriela's people had shown earlier.

The whole time Marlene watched this play in amazement, marveling at just how descriptive her daughter was, knowing exactly what she wanted and what she did not.

"I guess she wants you to do it," the woman in boots said, mirroring Marlene's thoughts.

The nurse in white asked Marlene, "Are you a registered nurse?"

"No, not at all," she responded.

Then the woman in boots looked pleadingly at the nurse in white.

"I am absolutely not supposed to do this, and if anyone outside this room finds out, I will lose my job and perhaps have to change my field entirely," she said, in a barely audible voice. "You can hold the needle, Marlene, but I will do everything else."

With that, Marlene took hold of the syringe, and the woman in boots helped Gabriela to hold still. Marlene took the alcohol swab and rubbed it on her daughter's arm. The child did not flinch. Then she pointed the needle at the injection site. But when the nurse in white moved her hand so that she could plunge the needle into the arm, Gabriela began to scream and curled up in a ball under the table.

"Okay, you win, Marlene. If anyone sees this, I am dead, and if you miss the spot, then there will be disagreeable repercussions. I will show you without a needle. I will mark exactly where to inject the vaccine with a pen."

The nurse took Gabriela's arm and made a bull's-eye on the skin with her pen. Gabriela watched this action with a seriousness in her face, not moving once.

"Okay," the nurse said, "take a breath, and just put it in."

Marlene, sweating profusely, took the needle, placed it on the pen mark on the arm, and with a swiftness and precision that she was not used to in herself, she plunged the needle into her daughter's arm. As if an entire orchestra gave its crescendo finale, violins and tympani soaring to heights that spelled success, she pulled the needle out, giving it to the nurse who had crossed herself beforehand. Then the woman in boots put a band aid on the spot where the shot had gone in, as Gabriela gave a tiny whimper.

The nurse mumbled something inaudible under her breath as she threw the needle into the biohazard container. She exited the room with the biggest sigh that Marlene had ever heard.

Gabriela took her mother's hand and walked with her to the door. She gave one last look at the woman with the boots, and with a skip in her step, she smiled as she pranced down the hallway. Marlene waved to the nurse in white, who looked at her gruffly, then managed a weak smile.

* * *

Gabriela's little brain continually investigated her surroundings and everything that transpired around her. With one quick glance, she knew who an ally was and who was her adversary. The nurse in white was the latter. It seemed she could see right through her plastic smile. There was a nurse at the orphanage, known as Ludmilla to the speaking staff. To Gabriela, she was a monster whose only mission in life was to inflict pain on others. In Gabriela's mind, she held all kinds of syringes, her reason for being as she walked those dim corridors. Without knowing the word, Gabriela knew this woman was a sadist. The child knew that if she screamed loud and hard enough and hid herself so tightly in the corners of rooms, under tables, prepared to kick and or bite at any given moment, then she could escape the tortures that the monster wanted to inflict on her. She learned that survival was what mattered, and to survive there were things you just had to do.

As soon as she saw the nurse in London, everything became triggered, and a kind of fire hit her brain, a fire that spelled out *Survive and do what you must do to avoid being pricked by a needle that a monster inflicted.*

And then there was the woman in the boots with the wild hair. She was an ally. She understood. Her mother, she was the biggest ally of all. As she held onto the hand of the woman who was now her mother, she felt again that surge of love, attachment. She would never leave this woman, and this woman would never leave her. She would make sure of this. Fires got extinguished when this woman with the big hands was near her. She clamped onto this big hand, keeping it in hers, willing this hand to never leave hers. Ever.

The two followed the queue that would enter the biggest airplane that this little child could ever have imagined. She had no idea where this airplane would be going, though perhaps she sensed it would be very far away. Maybe she knew, dimly, that she would not return for a very long time to the place that had been her home since birth. She was not old enough to know about different languages, differing customs; she was not mature enough to understand the abstract concepts of life. But what she did perceive was that this was a big, a very big moment for her in her little life, and she paid attention to every single detail as it was happening. She was excited; she was ebullient. Underneath her watchful gaze at all the little nuances around her—the people's expressions, the buttons on the seats, the shoes the flight attendants wore—underneath all these significant things in the mind of a young child, she was beyond happy. She was filled with an enthusiasm that made her smile, made her mother smile, and together the two started this grand voyage with incessant giggles as they wrapped their arms around each other and cuddled. Gabriela sat on Marlene's lap, ensconced in her smells of sweat and lavender. When she returned to her own seat at the window, her seatbelt buckled tightly around her, the plane took off and soared. She stared out the window, whose view stretched out for an infinity. Life was this, she thought, all of this, as she closed her eyes tight. Then she opened them again and let the clouds and the sky and everything around her fill her with delight.

CHAPTER TWENTY-TWO

"What we have here is a cello made by Francesco Rugeri, dated 1680. Rugeri was quite possibly an apprentice of Amati from Cremona, Italy. The simple poplar wood he used, which made his instruments look beat up, gave it away. In a novice's view, they have no value. In short, here is one of the finest masterpieces that has ever been created in the world of the cello."

Collective sighs filled the room; Thérèse, Jakub, and Philippe sat back and gawked at the marvel sitting in front of them.

Thérèse's heart was beating fast as she gazed at the piece of wood that she had brought in just that morning. She had not slept in two days, her hair was an unwieldy mass of strands, and she stank. No one at that moment, though, looked at her or paid attention to her odor. All that mattered was what was in front of them, a cello that had survived more than three centuries.

"Play it, please," Jakub pleaded, breaking the spellbinding silence.

Philippe picked up the burnt umber bow, itself a masterpiece, and sat with the cello nestled between his legs. He stroked the strings and played a simple scale.

"I am anxious, shaking," he commented. "Never in my life have I heard such a sound."

"Continue. *Please.*"

He began with Ernest Bloch's *Suite No. 1* for solo cello. The haunting notes, each one pulled out with angst by the bow, re-sounded in that room, the sound not only an epitaph for the dead, the ones lost in war, but also a connection to the living, to the moment where the notes sank into the heart and lay there, stroking it.

Then he moved to Bach's *Suite No. 1*. The notes lifted off the cello as if they could fly. The movement of the bow on the strings was so effervescent that only a master cellist could accomplish such transcendence.

For thirty minutes he played the Rugeri, and for those thirty minutes hardly a breath was taken, as the instrument came alive. It seemed to know that it was free again, as if it had a conscious self that it would be, once again, played to its fullest capacity, the way the maker had intended.

When Philippe finished, silence filled the room, and only then could one hear the pattering of rain on the windows. Eyes were wet with tears, the notes still reverberating in the ear and the soul of each listener.

After many minutes, Jakub got up and went over to the case and peered inside. He then pulled up a piece of the velvet that lined the wooden box and found what his dreams were seeking. There, in a folded piece of paper, tattered and thinned, were the words "*Solomon Herschel… 868, rue des Paysans Riches 75016 Paris.*"

He then silently, purposefully, walked to the huge binder on his desk.

"Mr. Herschel died, alongside his wife Emilie, in Auschwitz, February 1942."

Then he went to his second binder.

"Solomon Herschel was the principal cellist in L'Orchestre National de France."

The two men and the woman stared at the cello. Their eyes fixed on the wood, the strings, the curves and lines that interconnected. When the last few words hit them, a collective sigh filled the room as their hearts became heavy with grief.

Jakub looked at his third thick binder. The papers were loose, untamed, and stuck out in all directions.

"There is one survivor from this family, a woman by the name of Amélie Klein, the granddaughter. She lives in Auckland, New Zealand."

CHAPTER TWENTY-THREE

The Golden Gate Bridge shot up like fire coming from the depths of the sea.

Marlene sighed. She—now they—were home.

As the plane dipped bravely toward the Pacific Ocean, the wings a mass of brilliance, Marlene noticed her feet were tapping on the floor, as if she were about to dance down the aisles with exuberance. She grasped Gabriela's hand as they both looked out the window at the crystal-blue day. The sun twinkled from the west onto the expanse of ocean that lay unencumbered in front of them.

With no bags to retrieve, their exit from San Francisco International Airport was a simple act of breezing into the taxi that took them up Highway 101 into the city. At first, Gabriela's head bounced into a series of nod-offs. Jet lag hit her full-on, but as soon as the car exited the freeway and maneuvered its way down Fell Street, her eyes popped open and her face pressed into the glass. She stared at the rows of Victorian houses that lined every road as they approached Golden Gate Park. As the car turned left onto Duboce Street, Marlene's heart leaped in a thousand and one directions. She had gone this way so many times, but never in her life had she felt this much excitement at the prospect of home so close. She had only been gone a few days, but it felt like a decade. In those few days, she had matured, somehow. She clasped onto the child that would be with her for the rest of her life. She now experienced the feeling that she mattered to someone and that someone mattered to her. Maybe it was all the jet lag, lack of sleep, excitement, but it took everything in her to try control the urge to weep, to let out these feelings that swam through her. The taxi arrived at her apartment, and they got out.

Marlene looked over at her daughter, who had let go of her hand and appeared absorbed in the neighborhood in front of them. She skipped and hopped in the front yard, and then got on all fours and clambered through the bushes, following the neighbor's cat, a ginger tabby with no tail. She seemed to immediately become its friend. It played a "follow me everywhere" game and made sure that Gabriela was within sight. Marlene stared at the two and smiled and felt the naturalness of this game, a cat without judgment, a Deaf child who had just landed in a strange world who needed a friend.

This is precisely why I love young children, she said to herself, *the pureness of it all, the universal expression of wonder, that look on their faces that expresses the joy in newness, in the art of discovery, in meeting new faces, in stomping in the puddles of life, untethered by the myriad expectations that present themselves only later in the human existence. Gabriela will be fine,* continued her inner monologue, as she wiped the tears off her face and smiled, while her daughter, absorbed in the cat, laughed and muttered unintelligible sounds that somehow the cat seemed to understand.

* * *

Gabriela had made her first friend. She had seen cats when she was tiny, stray ones, wild and cumbersome in this wildness. To her, they were mean, and she put them on her *Do not trust* list after she had made several attempts to befriend them, only to get clawed viciously until blood had oozed everywhere.

This one was different, this one that did not have a tail. It had a face that was friendly, and therefore Gabriela put this cat on her mental list of those to be trusted. When she talked to it, it understood her, and so far, no human had been able to do that. She loved playing hide-and-seek with this orange-striped cat that was her first friend in her new home. But then a big dog came by on a lead. It tore away from its unhappy-looking owner and chased her new friend up a tree. Gabriela realized her playtime was over, and she ran to her mother, cheeks flushed, and grabbed her hand. They went up the stairs, and her mother had a key that she turned around and the door opened. Immediately, walking over the threshold, Gabriela smelled something that made her feel welcome. She did not know what the smell was, kind of like the earth, she thought, or maybe something like old wood that she recalled from when she was very tiny, and she crawled around on the floor in her first home before she went to the big home. It smelled good, this new smell, and whatever it was, she liked it. She said to herself, *I will never leave this smell. It is mine now.* Then, her mother led her to a room with a little bed in it. It was full of stuffed bears and a quilt. Gabriela looked puzzled when she entered the room. She did not feel like she belonged in it. She walked out, and then, next to the room with the bears was another room with a bigger bed and no bears. Instinctively, she skipped over to this bed and plopped herself on it and sighed. This was the bed where her mom slept. She would sleep here too, she decided. Marlene smiled as Gabriela sprawled out on the bed. Marlene took off her shoes and her daughter's. First one, then the other gave a big yawn, and then one and then the other fell fast asleep, their hands interlocked as the cat outside climbed down the tree and looked around for his new friend.

* * *

The sun poured through the bedroom window as Marlene opened her eyes to the warm breath of her daughter, still fast asleep. She got in the shower and washed off the scents of travel. As she soaped herself, she began to feel completely exhausted. She toweled off her hair, returned to the bed, and sank into a half day's sleep, while Gabriela's body did not move once in the bed. Sometime around 3 p.m., they both opened their eyes, groggy still. Each was covered with moisture.

Gabriela, still in a dazed state, had wet the bed.

Marlene cradled the small child in her arms and brought her to the shower, where the two submerged themselves in the flow of hot water, as they had at the hotel in Bucharest. Marlene shampooed the child's hair, put conditioner in, and after rinsing for several minutes, she turned off the water and wrapped her in a soft huge towel.

Gabriela walked around the apartment, and as she did so, the towel dropped to the floor. Seemingly oblivious to her nakedness, she ended up in the living room. She became engrossed in a book about cats that she found on the shelf. She kept one eye on the book and the other on her mother, who appeared to be preparing lunch in the adjoining kitchen.

Marlene had no idea what Gabriela liked to eat. So far, she had eaten everything that Marlene put in front of her with a zest that was more like desperation, something to fill the starved spaces. She cooked up scrambled eggs, toast with peanut butter and jam on the side, some slices of oranges and apples. She made a mental note to buy milk. This would be a staple from now on. *Shopping will take on a whole new dimension.* She loved her grocery store, and she could not wait to peruse the aisles for food for the two of them. The thought made her giddy. As she buttered the toast, she looked over at the little girl, naked and absorbed in her book. She went to the dresser she had prepared before she left and pulled out a pair of underpants and a selection of shirts, pants, and leggings, and threw in a skirt, not knowing how Gabriela wanted to dress herself. She laid these all out in front of her. Gabriela looked up and scanned the clothes. She picked up the underwear and put them on and then stared at the choices of clothes. She picked out an orange shirt, the brown leggings, and the orange skirt on top of those. Marlene noticed that the orange was the same color as the cat next door, Gabriela's new friend. Marlene smiled at her daughter's outfit choice. She helped her get the clothes on. She then reached out her hand, inviting her into the kitchen.

Gabriela sat down and grabbed a piece of toast with butter. Marlene handed her a spoon, opened the jar of peanut butter, and let her daughter sniff the contents. The child put the spoon on the table and instead put her entire hand in the jar, licking her fingers and her palm filled with peanut butter. She smiled as she again plunged her hand in the jar. When she was done, her entire face was aglow. Peanut butter mixed with her smiles that made Marlene laugh and laugh as she got out a dishcloth and proceeded to wipe clean the amber substance that covered Gabriela's hands and face.

The meal over, Marlene changed the sheets on the bed while Gabriela went to the extra bedroom and pulled out all the bears. She lined them up in the living room, one by one. She made sounds to them, and she had them all eat from a pretend jar of something that Marlene suspected was peanut butter.

The phone rang.

Marlene picked up the phone and heard a familiar voice.

"Hola!"

"Ciao!" Marlene answered the familiar greeting of her coworker, Juanita.

"Tell me everything!"

Marlene opened her mouth, wondering how to describe what had just happened in her life over the past week.

"No, don't bother talking," Juanita interrupted, reading Marlene's mind. "Just bring her in. Like *now*. We absolutely must meet her. We are all dying to set eyes on that kid."

"She's Deaf. Completely."

"Well, good, that will make us shut up for a change. We could use a quiet child to teach us." She laughed at her own joke.

"Oh, she can make quite a sound. Just you wait," Marlene laughed.

"Oh, I'm sure she can. Probably louder than any of us here."

They both guffawed.

"So, get some shoes on that child and walk your little selves over here. The kids are just waking up from nap. We've missed you."

"Missed you too, girl. Okay, we'll be right there."

Marlene got off the phone and sat down next to Gabriela. The bears were now napping all together in a heap.

Marlene had in her hand a pair of tennis shoes and a sweatshirt, which she handed to Gabriela while pointing at the door with her eyes. Gabriela put on the shoes, smiling, and left the sweatshirt on the floor as she ran to the door. Holding her mother's hand, she ran down the steps, looking for the cat. Seeing it was nowhere this time of day, Marlene pointed in the direction of the school.

Ten minutes later, children surrounded Gabriela, some her own age, some younger or older. Some slept, some were awake, some were peeing, some were getting their diapers changed, some were drawing, and some built with blocks. Some were getting their shoes on, ready to go outside.

"So here she is!" Juanita came up and put her hand warmly on Gabriela's head.

"God, you didn't tell me that you got a beauty queen while you were away!"

Marlene smiled as a half-dozen children ran up to her and hugged her.

"We missed you!" they cried out, nuzzling her.

"I missed you too. But look who I have now—my new daughter. She can't hear, as her ears don't work like yours. But her eyes work fine, and you can show her things without talking."

"Can she talk?" one of the children asked.

"No, when you can't hear, it's kind of hard to talk. She makes sounds, and that is her way of talking. But it's not the kind of talking you and I are doing now."

Some of the children stood quietly, absorbing this new information. A few others took her by the hand and led her, as if she were a doll, toward the block area to show her the towers they were building. Gabriela's eyes tensed up, and she ran over to her mother and clutched her hand. Marlene stopped and stroked her head, and they walked over together to the block area. Gabriela kept one hand in her mother's and used the other to stack blocks as she immersed herself in parallel play with the other children.

She began to make a house. First, she set up the foundation using the rectangular blocks. One by one, she pulled out all the large rectangular blocks from the shelf. She carefully lined each one next to the other with an architect's precision. Another child, next to her, was also making a building. He looked over at Gabriela's house, and when she appeared to not be looking, he took one of her long, rectangular blocks. She scowled at him and grunted and took back the block.

"But you have all the blocks! That's not fair!" he yelled. His hands were ready to tear at her hair, his nails ready to claw at her skin.

Marlene approached, feeling both her daughter's frustration and the other child's. She did not know sign language, and she wanted desperately for all of them to forge a common language to help facilitate communication.

She put one hand on the other child's back, and one hand on her daughter's.

"But she took all the blocks," he reiterated. "I want some too, and she isn't sharing."

"Let's see how we can fix this," Marlene suggested. "Gabriela is new here, and she doesn't know how things work yet, and you do. Maybe you can show her, without using words, how to work this out."

"Why can't we use words?" the child asked.

"Because Gabriela's ears don't work like yours. So, because of this, she can't hear the words you use."

The child looked at Gabriela, and she looked back at him. In that moment, no adult help was needed, and the nonverbal, almost primitive communication common between young children swam like a fish, free and unencumbered. They continued to stare at each other, and what transpired between them was mostly indecipherable for Marlene, but at the end of the stare, they both began to giggle, as if they had shared some private joke, some intimate moment that allowed all barriers to be broken. Gabriela handed a rectangular block to the little boy, and together they made a house. One by one, the two created a foundation, walls, windows, and a roof, and then, they gathered up all the stuffed animals in the room, and with the animals sitting around them, they continued to build, all without words. They created a little nest for themselves and their stuffed children.

This process went on for around thirty minutes. Marlene asked her colleagues to come over and observe. The teachers gawked at the focused play without making a sound.

"Wow," Juanita whispered to Marlene. "It just goes to show that compassion sure goes a long way."

"Hm. Hmm."

"Language is fluid, you know. It goes beyond words. Way beyond all the unnecessary verbiage that we adults put into things."

Marlene was speechless, nodding.

"This reminds me of when I first came to this country and didn't know a word of English. I needed friends so bad. At four, I already knew this, and so I had to do what I had to do. And I did exactly what these two just did."

Marlene looked at Juanita and smiled and put her hand on her back, seeing the tears subtly emerge in her colleague's eyes.

"We need to teach all these kids sign language," Juanita whispered.

"I was thinking the same thing. We've got to learn it first. It's us adults who are the slow learners."

Juanita laughed. "We have a staff meeting tomorrow. Can you be there? Let's bring it up."

"I'm technically off until Monday, but absolutely I'll be there. Do you want to talk tonight on the phone, and we'll come up with a plan?"

"Yes, call me when you're free. You know me, I am awake and awake and awake."

Marlene laughed as Juanita walked outside.

* * *

"And our third thing on the agenda was just brought to my attention this morning. First off, a big welcome back to Marlene who was terribly missed, but now, as we all saw yesterday, has brought back a jewel of a daughter."

Susan, everyone's favorite preschool director, smiled warmly at Marlene, who blushed.

"How about if you and Juanita describe your idea to all of us?"

The church basement meeting room was energized. By that point, everyone had met Gabriela and had heard of the new plan.

"All right, guys," Juanita began, the familiar lilt in her body telling everyone she meant business. "Starting this evening, we are all going to learn ASL, which means American Sign Language. We're going to learn it so well that we will start having sign language dreams."

Everyone snickered.

"It doesn't have to be fancy, and we don't have to learn at a level to talk about politics or poetry, but we do need to learn as much as or more than our children here at school. Because…" she turned to Susan.

Susan smiled and took the floor. "Because we want to turn this school into a sign language full immersion preschool, where parents can come from all over the Bay Area to bring their children. Not only will this school be the only one in the Bay Area doing this, but through this, we will build a huge profit base for this school. It's a win-win solution. And we are going to start tonight, first with a vote of confidence, and then with our first lesson. We have brought here a video of sign language learning for young children. Every teacher will get one of these videos, and we will have extra lessons at every one of our staff meetings."

"Excuse me, can I interrupt here?" the usually shy Leslie asked.

"Sure."

"I think this is the most marvelous idea that has ever come up in this school."

Marlene and Juanita smiled. "Thanks," they said at the same time. "Maybe it's a good time to ask if there are any other comments or questions?"

"I know a bit of sign language," Rudolfo interjected. "Can I bring in what I know and use it with the kids?"

"Yes! In fact, teach us a bit now, if you can," Marlene said, excitement exuding from her.

Silence filled the room as all eyes turned to Rudolfo, the dashing intern from San Francisco State University whom the children affectionally called Rudolf the Red-Nosed Reindeer.

He took his hand and touched the side of his forehead with

the fingertips. He then extended his hand out in the air.

"That means 'hello.'"

Everyone tried. Giggles filled the room.

His fingertips then touched his chin. He moved his hand away from his face and waved, much like the queen's wave.

"That means 'goodbye.'"

Again, everyone imitated him, the giggles getting louder, as if they were young children who were learning something terribly exciting for the very first time.

The lesson went on for thirty minutes.

"This is fabulous! We need to move on, though, so we can end the meeting in time. I have a few more agenda items to discuss." Susan smiled. The expression on her face was ebullient.

After the meeting, the energy was decidedly different in the school. As the teachers got up to leave, they were all bubbling with enthusiasm, ready to begin communicating in ASL with the children the next day.

* * *

Progress notes:
Student: Gabriela Robinson (birthday 12/15/1981)
Teacher: Rudolfo Ricci
11/29/1985

I would like to write these notes from what I have observed in her preschool classroom…plus what I wonder about with this child. Gabriela fascinates me. She has been at this school for ten months. She is profoundly Deaf (since birth). She is now fully immersed in learning ASL. We began this process the day she arrived, three months ago. (Our school is transitioning into a fully immersive ASL preschool.)

Part of these process notes are maybe what she is thinking. Observing her makes me want to delve into the study of Deaf language acquisition. I put what I imagine she is thinking in quotation marks.

"Everyone is waving their hands in the air, all around me. They look so funny. They make me laugh. I still prefer the kids who just look at me. Without all those silly hands, up and down and all around. I love my mom's lap the most. It's soft and warm and I fit just perfectly. Other kids want to sit there too, and I have to share, and I don't like to do this. Other kids open their mouths a lot. I don't know what's happening, but I kind of do, because I look at their faces. There's a boy in the room. He doesn't talk much. He doesn't use hands that wave around. But his smile is nice. And he shares his blocks with me. At first, I didn't want to share with him, but then I changed my mind, and it was fun when I did. We make homes with blocks and put all kinds of things inside. Then we live there. We laugh a lot. There's a teacher I really like. Sometimes he picks me up and swings me around, and we laugh together. He opens his mouth, and he waves his hands, but he doesn't make me wave my hands if I don't want to. He's just nice. Sometimes this teacher makes lunch for us. He loves this stuff that's long and skinny, and it slurps in your mouth. He showed us how to twirl it around the fork, and sometimes it falls on the ground. And the stuff you put on top is like tomatoes and it is so yummy."

Gabriela is an easygoing child. Sometimes she signs to herself, and every day I can see her brain in motion as she begins to learn to communicate. When she gets frustrated, she runs to her mom and sits on her lap. If her mom's lap is not available, then she makes a grunting noise, and then comes over to me and I make a lap for her. She sits there for a few minutes and proceeds with her play. She seems to have one best friend, a boy who has little verbal language. They do parallel play sometimes, but mostly do some good cooperative play in the block area. Their communication is silent, and they laugh a lot together. She is curious about everything in the preschool. She spends a lot of time observing others. She is very imaginative in her play and expresses many feelings through the make-believe situations that she conjures up. She seems very adaptive to change. Except for her one friend, she doesn't spend a lot of time with the other children yet, as they are just beginning to learn ASL and forget to use it. She is quite independent in her choice of play. She has a great appetite and sleeps well at nap.

* * *

Progress notes:
Student: Gabriela Robinson (birthday 12/15/1981)
Teacher: Rudolfo Ricci
11/25/1986

Over the past year, Gabriela has progressed immensely in her cognitive, language, and social development. Also, over the past year, all the children and staff at our center have become completely bilingual with ASL and spoken English. This language fluidity has proven to be an exceptional tool in language and concept comprehension for Gabriela. In addition to manual language, everything in our school has a written label, so that all the children can identify objects with the written word that describes it. Gabriela has a fascination for books and stories and wants to be read to constantly. She especially loves to sit on a teacher's lap and have stories and books around her that the teacher reads to her with ASL. While she used to sit alone and sign to herself, now she is interacting almost constantly with other children and adults in ASL. She is a very happy child and laughs often with other children. Her sense of curiosity has not wavered, and sometimes she and other children will explore things in the classroom that call for this fascination with discovery. She maintains an active imagination, as seen through her play and the pretend characters she manipulates. She has a love of animals and enjoys observing them in their natural habitats. From little insects that burrow in the garden, to birds that fly overhead and sometimes land on the trees outside, to a neighbor cat she told me about, she expresses a fascination with

* * *

A Little More Than One Year Later

January 1987

Kids open their mouths a lot. I wonder what sound is. I look at
faces. I wonder what this must be like. One day, will I wake up
and open my mouth and then sound will come out? I have had
a best friend since when I came here. He doesn't open his mouth
much. We play without that. His name is Riley. He can tell me
things with his hands. Sometimes we fight over things, like which
block to use in our pretend homes we make. But then we end up
laughing. He smiles at me, and I smile at him. All the kids use
their hands to talk. They call this ASL. It seems that girls all open
their mouths more than boys do. There's one girl, she has different color skin, it's darker, it's like chocolate. This girl has a nice
smile, and sometimes we play, we run around, and we laugh. I like
that. She is my friend. She comes to my house for playdates. We
get to play with my toys, and then we play with the neighbor cat.
He is an orange cat, and his name is Galileo. He doesn't have a
tail because the doctor cut it off when he had an accident when
he was little. I and my friend—her name is Shantay—play games
with him and follow him around. Shantay told me he doesn't
purr like a regular cat and makes a funny sound instead like an
old man clearing his throat. I have a favorite teacher. Ever since I
was really little, he picks me up and puts me on his shoulders and
swings me around. He laughs and I do too. He opens his mouth a

lot with the other teachers, but with other children and especially with me, he talks with his hands. He told me he was born in a place called Italy. He said Italy is very close to where I was born. He likes to cook things like spaghetti. When I was super little, he showed me how to eat it like a grown-up. So, my favorite food in the whole world is this stuff that is gooey. It's called peanut butter. At home I get to put my whole arm in the jar. It makes my mom laugh. So, my mom. Have I told you about her? I love her. She loves me. I always know this. Every single second of my life I know this. It's like she has put the sun around my head, and it is warm and happy.

CHAPTER TWENTY-FOUR

Three years later

1990

Essay: What does deafness mean to me?
by Gabriela Robinson
Assignment for Mrs. Burgee, Third Grade
California School for the Deaf, Berkeley

I could say that being Deaf is wonderful. And I could say that being Deaf is horrible. Both are true. There are days when I really don't even think about it. It just is. And that is true too. It's like having ten fingers and ten toes. It's just a part of me, so why spend time thinking about it? But this is an assignment, and I always do my assignments.

I think it's harder now that I am older. At first, when I came to the United States, a lot of other kids my age didn't have much language, so I wasn't that much different. Sometimes the hardest part of being Deaf is not about being Deaf but being so different from the rest of the world. And who wants to be so different?

Now I am in Berkeley, at a great school where everyone is Deaf. You'd think this would be easier, and in some ways it is, because we're all Deaf here. And every single day we are signing, and our hands are flying out of the sky, racing around, and everyone here talks with their hands. So that's cool. It's like we have this very

*special place where we're not different. We're kind of all the same,
but we're not, of course, because each of us looks different. Some of
us are what's called profoundly Deaf—that's my category—and some
of us are mildly Deaf. And then there are all those in between. But
we don't think of those categories. We're just Deaf. And the school is
really good in not making any of us learn how to lip-read and try to
"not be Deaf" and mix in with the hearing world. It's Berkeley, after
all, the birthplace of the free speech movement!*

*But then there's the other side of the coin. Do you remember I
said that being Deaf is horrible? Well, it is, in some ways. Because
it means that most of the world has absolutely no idea how to communicate with you. It means that on a Saturday, when school is
out, and you want to go shopping with your mom, you have got to
depend on her to talk to people about what you want. You can't just
go up to the counter, with your own money you have saved from
your allowance, and tell the clerk, "Please, ma'am, I'd like to buy
this." Either you do it silently, and the clerk tells you that you owe
25 cents, and you can't hear her, or you've got to ask your mom to
do the whole thing. And that's really hard sometimes.*

*There was one time that I really hated being Deaf. My mom told
me if I want to talk about it in this essay I can. I don't really want
to, though.*

*Thank God I've got a great mom. Some of the people in my school
don't have great moms. But I do. And I'm lucky. Every day I feel
I'm lucky because my mom is there. She's like my rock. She makes
being Deaf not so hard, when you think about it. She kind of turns
the horrible around and makes me just happy inside no matter what
or who I am.*

* * *

Gabriela never wanted to go to Orange County that weekend,
but she adamantly refused the option of staying with a friend and
her family in Berkeley. At eight years of age, she still clung to her

mother as her rock. The thought of being away from her brought up too much anxiety, flashbacks of the orphanage where she hid in corners and under tables and felt left and abandoned—a part of her life that would haunt her always.

Marlene, who had been a teacher's aide in her daughter's classrooms since the first year she arrived at the School for the Deaf, had to attend an annual teacher training. This was usually held in San Francisco, but this year the trainer had a family emergency, and the weekend course would be given by his associate, who only did the training at the Happy Holiday Motel in Orange County. Both Marlene and Gabriela groaned at the thought.

"Well, it's either you stay at the motel with me and go to childcare while I am in class, or you stay with your friends here in Berkeley."

In a small voice, Gabriela said, "Orange County." Dreading both choices, she packed her small suitcase with mostly books and art pads, markers, and fine pencils. She decided she would lose herself in a quiet space and avoid at all costs the hearing world and their ugly ways toward Deaf kids.

Marlene decided to skip the meet-and-greet on Friday night, and they took an early flight Saturday morning from Oakland to Orange County, where they left the balmy days of early May in Berkeley to the stiflingly hot and dry and treeless Orange County.

Childcare was to be held in the motel lounge, a small bleach-infused room with a couch, TV, and adjoining pool area, which was a postage stamp–size bit of water that could hold up to five people. Gabriela approached the other three children and sized them up and down, immediately repulsed. She looked at her mom with pleading eyes.

"I can't take you to class," she signed. "I already asked. You'll be okay. You have all your books and your drawing pads. I'll meet you for lunch in just a few hours."

The person in charge of childcare was an Old Mother Hubbard type, a stout old lady with a penchant for soap operas, which she had blaring the entire morning. She occasionally looked over at the children without any real interest. The two other girls in the group watched Gabriela and Marlene sign and whispered to each other, immediately bonding. They skipped off outside and spent most of the day in and out of the pool and appeared to be ensconced in their play, purposefully excluding the one lone boy and the Deaf girl. The boy sported a ripped T-shirt that read "Kill" in bold letters. Blood-colored paint dripped down the front and back of the black garment that barely covered his middle. He had pulled his baggy pants down to his groin.

Gabriela took her seat on the couch next to Old Mother Hubbard. She decided she would stay there and not move a bit and hide away in her book. It was a big book, *The Complete Book of Fairy Tales from All Over the World*, four hundred pages long, and she thought now would be a perfect time to lose herself in make-believe stories that could take her away from her physical environment. One page, two, three, she was already up to page twenty when she noticed that the old woman next to her was wincing and holding her belly. It was her digestive system, calling for a toilet. With significant effort, she heaved herself up off the couch, and with a quick pace made it to the bathroom, where she would stay for quite a long time. Gabriela felt her breath become tight. She tried to read, but no words could register in her mind, and everything became a blur to her as she closed her eyes for a second and tried to will away her tension.

Everything after that happened so fast. These things always do. The boy stopped his incessant bouncing of a mostly deflated beach ball and sauntered into the lounge, grinning.

"So, your protector is gone. You poor thing, you don't have the old fart to take care of you. Oh, that's right, you're Deaf. You can't hear a word I'm saying. I could say anything I want to you, and you won't even know." He laughed, and spit came out of his mouth. He took the ball and threw it at Gabriela. She put out her hand and averted its landing on her face.

"Oh, so you can protect yourself, little Deaf slut, you. I better work harder then."

He ran over and grabbed her book and ran outside and threw it in the pool. "Now you won't have anything to read. Poor little Deaf girl." The girls in the pool giggled quietly.

"And you can't even tell me to stop. I like this. I should hang around you more often."

Gabriela felt bile in her throat, felt like she was going to be sick. Tears welled up that mixed in with the bile, and then she remembered. Remembered the boy when she was three, at the orphanage, the one with the scar on his cheek, the one who taunted her. She remembered hating that boy, and the one in front of her at that moment reminded her of the scarred one, and in her small body something gathered, a mixture of the present and the past and all those moments when she couldn't speak, couldn't defend herself, couldn't hear the taunting but saw their faces spewing out words that only spelled hatred. Her own rumblings became louder and louder, and she approached the boy with the Kill shirt and got closer and closer to him until she was at his eye level, and her hand tightened into a fist, so tight it could break a tree limb. Her fist flew up and hit his nose, and the other fist, even tighter, hit his groin. He fell and grabbed his balls. Blood from his nose spewed out everywhere.

The old woman emerged then from the bathroom and held her belly and groaned. She saw first the blood, everywhere, and then saw the boy on the floor writhing in pain.

"Oh God."

She picked up the phone and made two phone calls. Minutes

later, an ambulance and a fire engine roared up to the Happy Holiday Motel. As the paramedics strapped the boy to the gurney, an irate, distraught mother stormed through the door.

"What happened, honey pop? Oh, my treasure. What happened?"

"She lunged at me, that Deaf girl. Ow, Mom, I hurt so bad."

The woman looked over at Gabriela, her fists raised.

"Okay, ma'am," the paramedic said. "He's underage, so you're required to come into the ambulance with him. We're leaving now."

"But we must find out about this. This girl wounded my son."

"Ma'am, we're leaving now. Get in the ambulance, please."

"We'll get to the bottom of this, you despicable girl." Her eyes were like poison gas, emitting flames.

The old woman got on the phone again, and after the sirens had abated and the moaning child and the venomous mother were long gone, in ran Marlene, out of breath.

"It appears your daughter whopped him hard."

"It appears… What did you see?"

"I'm sorry, Mrs. Robinson, I was in the bathroom when it happened. I know I shouldn't have eaten all those rum balls for breakfast. I had a bad case of the runs. By the time I came out, it was all over. Blood everywhere. I am going to have a time of it to clean all this up."

"What happened?" Marlene signed to her daughter, who was slumped on the couch.

"I don't know what he was saying, Mom, but he had evil in his face. Huge evil. He threw my book in the pool, and I knew that was just the beginning. So, first I whopped him in the nose, and then in his privates."

"Oh God." She sighed. "Why the privates?"

"It just happened. I didn't think. I was so mad."

"I bet you were. What's done is done. Next time, though, some-times just one blow is all you need to get the message across to leave you alone. Then, if that doesn't work, you go to Plan B. You've got to use your brain as well as your gut feelings, as hard as that might be sometimes."

"I'm sorry, Mom."

"It was awful, what he did. I'm sorry you had to be in that horrible place."

They were all quiet.

"How about we help this lady clean up the mess she has all over so when tonight's guests come, they don't think a murder has happened here?"

All three took the rags the old woman had tossed on the floor, dipped them in bleach solution, and wiped up the red, making the floor and the furniture sparkling white all over again.

"Let's get out of here," Marlene suggested, her voice tired. "We'll grab some lunch at the airport, change our flight, and leave today." She looked at the old lady. "Can I please use your phone? I need to call the workshop presenters and tell them I had a family emergency and I need to leave early."

"Of course." The woman pointed to the phone at the front desk. After the call, the two headed outside. The sun burned their necks. The frenzied world around them blurred their senses as they held each other's hands and made their way to the airport.

By the time they arrived back home in San Francisco, the boy had been released from the ER. He had sustained only bruises.

* * *

Marlene looked at Gabriela, fast asleep on the sofa. The rain pounded outside, an incessant rhythm. She sighed, her teacup in hand, and watched the rise and fall of her daughter's chest.

After Gabriela had told her the whole story, Marlene had cried hard the night before in bed. The episode at the hotel was an episode no child should ever have to face. Marlene had wrung herself with guilt, remembering the pleading look on her daughter's face moments before the episode. *I should have taken her to class,* she repeated so many times it made her sick. In the middle of the night, her thoughts jumbled around, as if she were shuffling cards. *She's a tough kid, though. Look what she did. At age eight, she took on a lousy bastard. She punched him in the balls. He probably needed even more than that. Who taught her how to do this? Survival. She taught herself, most likely. My daughter is tougher than I ever was or ever will be.* Then her mind wrapped back around her first thoughts. *Ahhh...being Deaf is so hard, to have to rely on those "survival instincts," to not be able to hear a word that's been said, to always be in that stance of the victim.* Marlene cried some more, perhaps feeling the pain her daughter had experienced and would always experience in the hearing world. *It's a hard life. I knew this would be hard, the moment I saw her. Yet I knew that she had something amazing in her, resilience, yes, more than just toughness, more than just being able to punch an asshole in the balls. She has something in her that the world needs, this wisdom, this inner light that shows others how to survive anything and everything.* She gazed at her daughter then, a child who had infiltrated her heart like a fine sap, like lifeblood, filled with such vibrancy in her very being. *I would do anything for this child.* She continued to gaze at Gabriela, watching her chest rise and fall with the precision of a metronome.

Marlene sat back in her rocking chair, remembering when she had first brought Gabriela home and how she'd held her in her arms and rocked her in the chair she was now sitting in, how she noticed how the child, her child, could completely relax and snuggle up against her and fall asleep so easily.

Her gaze went to the window as she watched the passing storm land on the earth, a last wave of wind making its final sound, like a carillon in a rain-drenched desert. Her thoughts turned to Thérèse.

It always surprised her when they did this, when they focused her mind on that one day in her life, on that one person who would through follow her life, somehow. *What if…* She paused to stare at a single leaf that fell effortlessly to the ground. *What if we had met, talked that day, created something beautiful together, and then adopted this child, watching her grow, witnessing her magnificence… What if we were here together, folded in each other's arms, watching our daughter fast asleep on the couch?* Marlene stared at her hand and felt the wetness of a single tear that had come from her eyes that slid down her cheeks, her chin, and then dropped onto the hand that brushed it away.

CHAPTER TWENTY-FIVE

The song "Little Boxes on the Hillside," written by the late Malvina Reynolds, described the homes that lined up on the South San Francisco hillsides. As the plane made a sweeping descent to the San Francisco Airport, Thérèse stared out the window at these identical homes, mesmerized by the approach to the city she had always wanted to visit. Beyond the magnitude of the iconic Golden Gate Bridge, from high up in a plane San Francisco was a fairy-tale world, one where water and mountains and a multitude of bridges and organized little boxes that people lived in.

She stepped through the airport like a dancer, her small body flitting like a feather to the car rental agency. As she waited in line, her mind pinched itself in a state of quasi-disbelief. *I am in San Francisco.* And although she would be returning to this same airport a little more than twenty-four hours later, she banished that detail to the back of her mind as she focused on the violin that had brought her here. This was a place she had dreamed about since her childhood, and she wanted to soak in every second of it until she had to leave the next day.

It was 4 p.m., and the thrift shop in Berkeley closed at 6 p.m. Déjà-vu swam through her as gridlock met her on her approach to the Bay Bridge. She turned on the radio.

"An accident on Highway 101 has compounded the regular rush hour today… Stalled traffic on all highways will create a long drive home, wherever you are. How about some uplifting music?"

Thérèse understood English, sort of. She understood enough to get that this would be a slow drive to her destination. This was San Francisco, however, and even if she was entirely unfamiliar with rush hour driving in the Bay Area, she was entranced by this part of the world, the multitude of people who called themselves Californians. That, to her, had a ring to it. *Certainly, even these freeways are paved with gold, no?*

She looked up, and on one of the buildings, waving with abandon, the colors dazzling, was a rainbow flag. *It is June, the month of Pride, and I am in San Francisco.* She beamed.

Inch by inch she crawled forward in her spacious rental car. She fiddled with the radio. Not particularly impressed by the local classical station, she turned the dial to what seemed like a folk music station and heard her favorite, Joan Baez, and then the Indigo Girls. She turned the volume up to high and sang along as she approached the Bay Bridge. There, on either side, the Bay greeted her, boats, water, and sky that made her think of freedom, of flower children, of Pride marches, and of limitless possibilities.

I am a fool, but I love this.

Her attention turned back to the road after she got off the bridge. She began to panic. Decisions had to be made as to which lane to get in. To the right was Interstate 580 East, then there was Interstate 880 South, and then to the left was Interstate 80 East to Sacramento. *Sacramento, merde, where's that?* She looked over and saw a tiny sign with one word: Berkeley. She swerved to get on I-80 East. She had all kinds of maps sitting next to her that the rental car agency had given her, but there was no place to pull over to look at those nicely folded pieces of paper. As she drove, she heard several drivers honking at her. *No patience for a dreamy tourist from France.*

"University Avenue exit, University of California" read a sign farther down the highway. She swerved to take that exit and drove up University Avenue, happy to be off the highway. She realized she had been sweating like a pig during that entire freeway ordeal. She pulled over at a gas station and asked for directions from a man who was filling his tank.

"Excuse me, monsieur, where Chatook Avenue? I look for 8806 Chatook."

The man shrugged his shoulders.

Thérèse pulled out a piece of paper with the address.

"Ah, Shattuck," the man smiled. "Straight up University, left on Shattuck, and go about a mile or so."

Ah, Californians, they are even friendly at petrol stations. Thérèse had a glow about her as she got back in her car and started up the engine.

* * *

North Berkeley, just a mile or so from the UC Berkeley campus, had its own energy. After all, it was there that the foodie movement began, most specifically with Chez Panisse, one of the grand *chef d'oeuvres* of what later became "California cuisine," focusing on local ingredients and forging direct relationships with local farmers, ranchers, and dairies. The restaurant itself was the brainchild of Alice Waters, a world-renowned author and food activist.

Across the street from this famous landmark in the Gourmet Ghetto was the newly developed Cheese Board Collective, a worker-owned and -operated business that focused on cheese and pizza flavored with ingenious mixtures of ingredients., Lines around the block were common, and musicians often played for those in line waiting for pizzas.

Then there was the bookstore, one of Berkeley's favorites, Black Oak Books. Between those treasured walls existed a myriad of bound publications that mirrored the city's urgings for a literary world. Nothing would ever befall that store, Berkeleyans always hoped.

The new kid on the block, where once there was a never frequented store of mass-produced office supplies, was the endearing Out of the Closet thrift store where all proceeds went to AIDS and HIV research and treatments.

* * *

At 5:55 pm, Thérèse sauntered into the blazing pink store at the intersection of Shattuck and Vine Street. She was the last customer to be let in. She asked the woman at the counter about the violin that was brought in the day before.

"Oh, I think we sold it, a couple of hours ago," she replied nonchalantly.

"But that's not possible," Thérèse said, tension making her accent more noticeable. "The owner said he would save it for me. I came over from Paris just to get it."

"You did?" The woman looked at her as if she were a full-on fool.

Maybe Californians are not as nice as I thought.

"Let me go check in the back to see if there is another violin back there."

Thérèse nodded and looked around. *Still, I like this place. It's organized. It has good energy. Surely my violin is waiting for me.*

The salesperson locked the front door and got on the phone.

"Hi, there. What do you know about a violin that we were supposed to save for a Frenchwoman?"

"Mm-hmm… mm-hmm… mm-hmm. Where? Uh…I couldn't find it. Mm-hmm. But someone came in a few hours ago and bought that one. Mm-hmm…mm-hmm. Let me look."

The woman disappeared into the back room and returned to the phone.

Thérèse was sweating, fearing the impending doom the phone call might bring.

"Wasn't there. Where? Nope. Looked there. Mm-hmm. Mm-hmm… You did? Okay. Mm-hmm. Mm-hmm… Oh my. Okay. Hold on."

Again, the woman disappeared into the amorphous world of the back room. She was gone for more than five minutes. Thérèse could hear the man's voice on the other end. He kept sneezing and coughing. *Sounds like he has a nasty cold.*

The saleswoman reappeared, a violin in her hand.

"Here you go," she said simply.

Thérèse beamed and pulled out a wad of green paper from her pockets, handing all the bills to the saleswoman.

She looked shocked at the amount of money that Thérèse had just given her and thanked her over and over for her patience.

Thérèse pranced out of the thrift shop. Her hand closed around the handle of the violin case as if they had been measured to fit. Her tension gone, she smiled and watched the people around her. *Ah, California…*

Pizza. Yes. She bopped into the Cheese Board. The smells of freshly made crust and sizzling fresh cheese invaded her nostrils and made her want to lunge at a pizza.

She had to pee like crazy and went first to the bathroom at the back.

There was an open stall and a girl who was holding the door closed for another stall. The girl stared firmly at Thérèse's face as she entered the open stall and closed the door, letting it hang open a bit. There appeared to be no locks on either of the bathroom stalls.

Thérèse felt a flood of relief as she emptied out and flushed and left the bathroom. The girl came out and looked at her again as she left.

Marlene exited her stall, and Gabriela signed to her, "Mom, that lady with the violin didn't even wash her hands." Marlene gave her daughter a look that said *Yuck*, and the two of them laughed. Then she held the door so Gabriela could go in and pee.

Thérèse realized she did not have any money left after paying for the violin, but then remembered there was a bit of cash left in her jacket in the car. She left the café to get it and walked far down the street to where she had parked her car. Marlene and Gabriela had already left the bathroom and the café and were walking down the street in the other direction.

"Mom," Gabriela signed, a serious look on her face, "there's something about that woman in the bathroom."

"What do you mean?" Marlene signed back.

"I don't know. I'm not sure. Maybe we'll see her again somewhere. She had really intense eyes. Maybe she knows you. I don't know. It's weird."

Marlene smiled. "You just had a feeling about her?"

"Yeah. Something like that."

"Okay. The woman with the violin. Kind of a name of a book or something."

The two laughed and dropped the conversation, as Thérèse walked back into the café, bought her pizza, and sat down at a table where the sugar and salt packets had been placed in a circle around the pepper shaker.

Undoubtedly the work of a clever child. Thérèse looked around and saw no child there and assumed it was the project of the girl from the bathroom. The one who had stared at her.

CHAPTER TWENTY-SIX

Five years later

20 May 1995

*E*ssay: *What does life mean to me as related to my Deafness? How am I connected to the world around me?*

By Gabriela Robinson
Eighth Grade
Class: Social Sciences
Teacher: Mrs. LaFay
California School for the Deaf, Berkeley

Every five years this school asks its students the same question: what does Deafness mean to me? Now, this question is connected to the global perspective, to life as I know it, and the teachers are asking us to ponder how are we connected? Underlying this premise is the question...are we connected as Deaf students? These are all good questions. I looked back on what I wrote five years ago, and I could not even talk then about the abuse I suffered that day at the motel. Maybe I was just too immature to understand that on that day, everything in my life changed from what I knew it to be to what I know now to who I am at this moment.

I will never know what that ignorant, mean-spirited boy said to me, but I read volumes of information in his face and in his actions.

Once I recovered from the experience, I vowed to never let my Deafness stop me from being who I am, in making a statement in this world, in advocating for Deaf people. I saw, from that experience, how terribly easy it was to be a victim, to fall into the hands of an evil force. I could tell he wanted me there, as his puppet, to be the victim I refused to be.

The other day I saw a documentary about a group of children in England who were interviewed every seven years. The film is called Seven Up! The filmmakers had the notion that a child's basic personality is formed when they are around seven years of age, and in this film, they asked those kids all kinds of questions when they were seven to get a sense of who they were and how they walked on this earth. Then, they interviewed these people every seven years to see if these people had changed much in their personalities. Now, these "kids" are about thirty-five, and what is interesting is that their hypothesis is indeed true: for the most part, the grown-up version is like a spitting image of the seven-year-old.

My point is this: I am who I am as a person. Yes, a huge part of my identity is being Deaf, but it is only part of my identity. That eight-year-old in the motel was a Deaf girl, but also a girl who is strong and determined, and who connects with a world who embraces this. I have nothing to do with people who are prejudiced or mean. I am not on the planet to engage with them, except to let them know that I deserve just as much space as they do. My connection with others stems from compassion, something I learned from my mother the day she set eyes on me in that orphanage. If you look at me every seven years of my life, I will probably be doing the same thing: I will be showing the world my strength, my unwillingness to be a victim, and I will be showing the compassionate world my love.

Being Deaf has given me a special key to a unique world, a world that has communication that makes no sound. I find that as intriguing and mysterious as I do challenging. I remember five years ago I alluded to this reality in the first paragraph of my essay. I sometimes dream about the whole world being Deaf. It is my little fairy tale, being the norm, not the exception. I giggle with the thought that the world is silent, and people on the planet just move through their days without a sound. Meanwhile, being Deaf in this real world of ours means that I can weave myself into corners that maybe the hearing world cannot do. I can observe faces more succinctly, never taking for granted a person's expression, the subtle cues of the human existence. I look at eyes, for they are truly the windows to the soul. I imagine that hearing people waste a lot of time in verbiage, unnecessary words that take up a lot of space. Being Deaf cuts to the chase, letting me really get to the essence of a person's experience.

Because I refuse, though, to learn the old-fashioned lip-reading, I will always most probably feel a bit of—or maybe a lot of—exclusion in the world. This is a hard reality, for it means that I either must be around a hearing person to maneuver through difficult tasks, or else accept a certain amount of aloneness in the world—once I leave my school and my protected haven of Deaf inclusiveness. I know the reality is that only a small percentage of people know sign language on this planet. But the determined part of me will never let this fact stop me. I will overcome that obstacle, as I feel I am a person on this planet who can overcome any obstacle that comes my way.

In conclusion, my being Deaf is an identity piece that will shift and change over time, but the essence of me will not. I am happy with that. Someone once told me, "It is what it is." I feel that is true. Being Deaf just is. And for all the parts of our personalities, the parts we love and the parts we hate, and all the parts in between, we are who we are.

* * *

Marlene walked out of the travel agency holding airline tickets in her hands. She pondered her eloquent thirteen-year-old, whose mind always mixed philosophy, poetry, and still, a bit of the fairy tale.

"I want to go back to see my roots, to feel the soil," Gabrielle had signed earlier that week. She paused. "I want to see the orphanage, and I want to see castles."

"Is there anything else you would like to see and do?" Marlene seemed quite intrigued by her daughter's declaration. "Do you want to visit any other country in Europe?"

"No, save that for another time. For now, just Romania. And not even all of Romania. Just a bit of it," she signed back.

But then, six weeks before they were to embark on their trip, there was a listing in the classified section of the *San Francisco Chronicle*:

> *Come and work on a farm in Romania. Mature thirteen-year-old and older. Must be able to work hard. Few girls are accepted. Free room and board for the summer.*

Gabriela put the clipping under her pillow.

"Change of plans, Mom," she signed, as they were eating breakfast the next morning.

"As in?"

"Look at this." She produced the classified listing.

Marlene read the listing. She chuckled and signed back, "I bet the line 'few girls are accepted' must have prompted you to want to do this."

Gabriela nodded, smiling.

She wrote to the farm, pleaded with them, and convinced them that she (and her mother, of course) were right for their program.

"We will see you next month," they wrote back, along with their address.

"You did it again," Marlene signed a few weeks later, holding the letter written on a tiny piece of flimsy paper.

"Did what?" Gabriela responded.

"Convinced yet another person to go beyond what used to be the Iron Curtain."

They both laughed.

All they packed were work clothes and heavy boots. They scrapped the orphanage idea, and the castles too. Instead, the two would be harvesting wheat in a horse-drawn cart in Transylvania.

CHAPTER TWENTY-SEVEN

The sky was laden with thick clouds, swirling darkly around the plane, and turbulence infested the air. Thérèse thought she was going to be sick. *Please let this plane land.* Just that morning at 6 a.m., Jakub had phoned her, his voice insistent.

"I think it's a major find."

"But you say that often," she teased, her voice still heavy with sleepiness.

"*Oui.* That is true. But I do believe that this one could be a major historical discovery."

Over the years, Thérèse had learned to humor her colleague and supervisor. She adored this man and felt often like he was the father she had never had. There were times when she just wanted to call him Papa, smiling into the twinkle in his eyes that was reserved for the instruments, the only children he had ever known. He was quite secretive about his private life; she often thought he could be gay. He never mentioned a wife or even a girlfriend. Their conversation was solely devoted to music and instruments. Over the past ten years since she had begun this work, Thérèse had cherished every one of their interactions.

"I see there is a Grenoble–Lyon train that leaves in an hour. And then there is a direct flight to Bucharest that arrives at 3 p.m." Thérèse had become a genius at quickly figuring out transportation routes and times, using the stacks of pamphlets that she always had by her phone.

"Perfect. The shop closes at 4 p.m. on Saturdays." There was
a pause. "Oh, by the way, they apparently don't know you are
coming. I was never able to reach them. I don't think they have
a phone."

"So how do you know they have the violin, if they haven't
talked to you?"

"It's a bit complicated. I am happy to share with you when I
see you, but I don't want to take any more of your time now. You
must rush."

Thérèse giggled as she threw on her clothes and was out the
door, racing to Grenoble, excited about her next bit of sleuthing.

He is rather a mystery, that Monsieur Bernovitch.

The early summer sun already seduced the air with a soft tenderness, a gentle kiss on the cheek, a quiet plea for more.

* * *

Bucharest, a city she had never been to, was pulsing. A frenzied summer storm was on the horizon. Still playing notes from
the dirges of revolution, a slow recovery from one of its dark-
est hours in history, Bucharest itself splayed out in front of her
like a beautiful, damaged woman who was attempting to shed
the scars of abuse she should never have had to experience. As
Thérèse stepped into the taxi that wove its way through bustling
streets, cars maneuvering themselves through huge expanses of
urban roadways, she felt transported into a kind of wistfulness. It
seemed that the old and the beginnings of the new were merged.
Hopefulness burgeoned in the air. It was confusing to her, this
juxtaposition of a scandalous past and a present-day hopefulness,
an identity crisis that was not sure how to manage the demands
that were placed on it. She looked at the faces of the older people
on the streets, the hardened gazes, the lingering oppression, expressions hinting at the impossibility of freedom, and she compared

them to the expressions of the young people in their torn jeans and their oblivious approach to life, the limitlessness that they seemed to dictate in their lives.

While it only took a few hours by plane to get from Paris to Bucharest, once there she felt worlds away from the reality of Romanian life, from the notion of dictatorship and what it does to a people. She longed to find the connecting thread; a fine strand of silk interwoven in the fabric of humanity. She opened her mouth to speak to the cab driver but found her voice stymied. Her ignorance of the language permeated the silence. She clutched the Romanian French dictionary she had bought at the airport, feeling its uselessness in her hands. She was able to manage a *Vă mulțumesc* to the driver, thanking him with an accent that was un-intelligible as she slipped him extra money. While his expression was blank when she spoke, with the lei in his hands, he smiled broadly.

She approached the weathered building, a hardened cement structure that seemed to be all that was left of an inauspicious establishment. Barbed wire surrounded the property, and mangy dogs filtered in and out of the neighborhood, their blighted bodies showing disease and neglect. Thérèse looked at the small sign on the door, scrawled in faded black letters: Vechi Si Noi. Old and New. She then looked around the corner of the building and noticed a smaller sign that had become obscured by some overgrown bushes that probably had not seen clippers in more than ten years. *Orfelinat,* it read. *Oh my God, this used to be one of those dreadful orphanages I have read about.* She shuddered as she took a deep breath and opened the door. A sickening mixture of antiseptic smell, mold, and junk surrounded her. Dust and an occasional mouse flitted around the darkened corners. She looked up at the peeling paint on the walls and the floorboards that were loosened. She had the feeling that many feet had trampled them over the years. She looked down one of the rooms to its far end and saw a tiny handprint permanently painted on the wall. She gasped, feeling the closeness of a child, one who had been housed in this notorious building, waiting out the decimated destiny of her little life.

I wonder what happened to that little one?

A middle-aged man approached; his back hunched over. His skin displayed a roughness; callous shreds of arduous work enveloped his hands. He looked at Thérèse and scanned her face. He looked down at her boots.

"*Bună*," he greeted her, his voice gruff. He cleared his throat and went over to the sign on the door and turned it around. "Open" now became "Closed." He pointed at the sign, and his weathered hand made the motion for her to exit.

"*Vă rog... vioara. S'il vous plaît.*" Please. Violin.

Just then a heavyset woman came out from the back. A dirty cloth hung from her forearm. She, too, looked down at Thérèse's boots.

Damn, I never should have worn these boots. She had bought them on a whim one day at a boutique on rue des Lilas in Paris. She never bought anything for herself, especially designer clothes. *What was I thinking, putting these on today?*

"*Ești franțuzoaică?*" You're French?

Thérèse flipped open her translation book and nodded. The woman winked at her husband, then turned to Thérèse and, with a brusque nod, implied that she could stay and get the violin. Her husband left for a moment, and in the silence, the woman pretended to dust the shelves. She mostly spread her filthy rag on each object, giving the items a black sheen. Her husband returned and produced a black case.

"Twenty-five thousand lei."

Thérèse gulped. She held out all the money she had exchanged at the airport. The man counted it and shook his head. His wife returned to the counter. Her cloth was even dirtier than before. She pointed to Thérèse's watch. Thérèse wanted to scream. It was her mother's watch, her most valuable possession. *These people are gauging me. Damn those boots. And why did I speak in French? I am an idiot.*

The man and his wife stared at the violin and shook their heads. They mumbled something to each other. Thérèse touched the gold band of her watch and felt tears well up in her eyes. As she stroked the smooth metal, a vision of a Romanian family arose in her brain. They were sitting down for the Pesach Seder, reading from the Haggadah. Candles were burning, and the sounds of a violin whispered in the room as the father played. The minor notes gripped at the heart. *This violin could have belonged to this family who perished in the gas chambers.* Her fingers then undid the clasp. The sleek metal passed from her hand to the wife who grabbed the watch and squeezed it in her bulbous hands. Then her husband extended his hand. He smiled. In that smile his face showed what his country had done to him. It revealed the pain and anguish, the abuse, the torture, yet on that face there was resilience, reflecting a culture that was able to be impervious to the ills of a political world. As Thérèse took his hand and shook it, there was in that moment something infinite—a human connection in a plagued world.

With the violin case gripped in her hand, Thérèse stepped out of the shop into the bleakness of the street. She began to run along the uneven concrete. Litter was strewn everywhere. She was not sure where she was even going. Silently she screamed out for her mother, as the summer storm unleashed water everywhere and blanketed her steps, the sidewalks, the world around her just trying to survive.

* * *

Monsieur Bernovitch unveiled the thin velvet that covered the violin. He handed the violin to Philippe, who scoped it with his magnifier.

He squinted. "There's writing here."

He put on his other glasses with more magnification, as he shone a brighter light into the instrument, near the F-hole. He wrote down the Romanian words, and after consulting his translation book, he gasped.

"What?" the other two asked, breathless. "What does it say?"

"To my darling Codoi, my Elena. Your Nicolae."

"As in Ceausescu?"

"Looks like it. That was his term of endearment for her."

"Oh my God."

"As history has it, she always wanted to play the violin. As a child, her family was too poor for things like that."

Philippe continued his research into the depths of the violin. His face contorted again, this time even more.

"I am holding the Lady Blunt Stradivarius, one of the world's most valuable violins."

Jakub ran to his books and thumbed through them with a frenzied gulp. "It belonged for a time to Georges Enescu, Romania's esteemed violinist and composer. Right before the Soviet occupation of Romania and his subsequent flight to Paris, it was said he gave this violin to his beloved student, Schlomo Lerner. Mr. Lerner became the country's most beloved musician, blending folk and classical into a seamless stroke of the bow. Within a year of receiving this violin, he was sent with his wife and his eight-year-old son to Auschwitz. His son is his only survivor, living in Vancouver, first violinist with the Vancouver Symphony Orchestra."

They were silent as Philippe played one of Enescu's Romanian rhapsodies. The image of the sunrise over the sweeping mountains of Romania filled the air, darkness turning to light in just that moment.

CHAPTER TWENTY-EIGHT

A cool rain greeted them. At the airport, a violinist played Romanian folk songs, a blend of minor melodies with a beat that made Marlene dance around her daughter. Gabriela looked slightly embarrassed, and her mother stopped dancing, but she could not stop glancing at the smile on her daughter's face, the lightness in her steps. She stared at her daughter, now an adolescent, strong, outspoken, passionate, and beautiful, back in the country of her birth. Gabriela beamed and looked around, watching the people around her. She laughed, signing.

"I wonder who is happier to be back?"

"I'm just seeing how far you've come since we were here last."

Gabriela smiled and grabbed her mother's hand and twirled her around as the violin continued the minor and major keys with a dissonance and a rhythm that made Marlene twirl faster as her daughter swung her around. A small crowd had gathered, and when the violinist finished the piece, applause erupted, and people threw coins into the violin case.

"I didn't know you liked to dance," Gabriela signed as they picked up their bags and wheeled them through the airport.

"You know, I didn't either." Marlene chuckled. "Maybe there is some intrinsic connection I have with this place where you were born."

"Hmmm. Maybe."

They boarded the train, and for most of the trip Gabriela was silent, staring out the window. Marlene was silent too and watched a world that felt altogether different than what she'd seen nine years ago. What she remembered was sketches of disarray, a chaos out of control, a world gone mad. As the train left the city and maneuvered its way into the lush countryside, the majestic mountains surrounded them. Around every turn, in every tunnel the train sped through, she sensed a resurgence, a pulsing life that had resumed.

After a long taxi ride from the closest station, they arrived at a beaten-down wooden house surrounded by fields and fields of wheat. Getting out of the taxi, they smelled fresh air first of all. The lightness of the rain brought out the tender shoots of grass, overgrown, at their feet. An old man, hunched over, smiled and greeted them. His hair, select wisps of gray, adorned his face, which displayed the fine wrinkles of an octogenarian. His wife, equally bent over, smiled profusely at the sight of the newcomers as she approached the mother and child. She extended her hand. That did not seem to be enough, and after the preliminary handshake, she pulled the child to her and embraced this being with Romanian roots. She then turned to Marlene and hugged her warmly.

"*Copil român frumos!!!*" Beautiful Romanian child!!! She kept pointing to Gabriela while smiling at Marlene. "*Frumos, frumos!*" Marlene was not sure what she was saying exactly, but it was surely complimentary. *I knew I forgot something. My Romanian-English Dictionary. It's there, sitting on my bed. I can't believe I forgot it. I was so busy dancing at the airport I forgot to buy one then.*

"Thank you," Marlene beamed back. They all hugged again. The almost ninety-year-old husband insisted on taking Marlene's bag as the elderly couple led the group inside the house. The smells were overpoweringly enticing, and lunch was ready. They all sat around the tiny rectangular table and ate stew and fresh bread. The house was simple, mostly dark with walls that badly needed a coat of paint. The furniture in the one room was sparse: one table, four old chairs, and a sofa that was tattered, torn, and faded.

The only sounds were those of slurping. The flavors of the stew reflected the age of the land, a country rich with history, a land that had been decimated by wars and takeovers, poverty, and loss. Food was life in that moment, and most probably in every meal that was cooked in that humble kitchen.

The woman and man gazed at Gabriela, who smiled as she ate. Without a word, she knew how to communicate to this couple everything they wanted to know.

After lunch, the couple showed them where they would sleep, in the barn on a bed of straw. As they showed Marlene and Gabriela their meagre offerings and gave them each a sheet and a tattered blanket, warmth filled their faces. Then they introduced them to the two old horses who would command the harvest. Then, with one last hug, they put their palms together, leaned their cheeks against them, and closed their eyes, indicating it was time for the siesta. They then left the barn.

"I love this place. I love these people," Gabriela signed. She curled up on the straw and fell into a deep sleep.

* * *

The moment the plane landed in Bucharest, she had known she was home. She sensed her mother knew it too. Her dancing. On the train she saw land outstretched, and she remembered the trip from her first home to the orphanage. She remembered the miles and miles of lush farmland. She remembered thinking: this is home. She did not know where her birth mother was taking her that day. She was so little. But she remembered feeling happy and sad. Happy because she knew this was home, and sad because she knew, at some level, she was leaving something. How did she know this? She was so little. All she knew was that on the train and then in the taxi, it had all come back to her. And then when the old man, and especially the old woman, met them and hugged her, she knew they were family. Was it the smell, or the warmth in their eyes, or the sounds of Romanian that she could not hear but felt, the ways their mouths moved when they talked, the ways they used their faces and their hands to communicate that level of warmth that just sank into her heart, her soul?

She did not care what kind of work they wanted her to do. She wanted to do everything for these two people. She saw her own birth mother in their faces. She saw her beauty, her pain, her anguish as she left her at the door of the orphanage.

* * *

"Okay. Your turn," Gabriela laughed and signed, as they combed and brushed the horses and let them rest after their long day of work.

All four became a team. They woke up early, with the 6 a.m. sun. Bread with jam and coffee for breakfast with the old ones at the table. Not much talk, mostly just smiles and laughter as each began their day. The old man assigned the tasks. He and the young ones would feed the horses and then hitch them up to the harvesting machine. Until noon the horses worked, and again in the late afternoon the three would be alongside them. All together they cut and gathered the wheat and established a rhythm that permeated the day. The wheat was their life, a gathering of life, sustenance that fed them, the village, and the neighboring towns. The old man whistled and hummed as he worked. Marlene and Gabriela were quiet and looked up every now and then and let the lushness of Transylvania nourish their bodies. The curve of the mountainous hills embraced them as the freshness of the air bathed them. Every muscle ached at the end of the day, an ache neither had experienced before. Gabriela did not seem to mind, and every time Marlene looked over at her daughter, she caught a smile she had never seen before, a smile that seemed to come from a very deep longing.

On Saturdays, the old man went to market to sell his grains of wheat, dried and finely pounded and sorted by his wife, a task she did every single day, except on Sundays. On market days, Marlene and Gabriela helped her and did other tasks around the house. They painted the walls, fixed cracks, swept the dirt floors, and helped cook the meals.

Days slipped into weeks with a feeling of timelessness, as finally the rhythm began to change, from the subtle to the obvious, the position of the sun, the fading light.

The summer was coming to an end.

Suitcases packed, Marlene and Gabriela stood in front of the old house. The hugging did not stop. Neither did the kisses on the cheeks. Their faces all showed tears. Then the taxi came and whisked the two away to the station. The train meandered along rivers and mountains, through a country seemingly unblemished, as Marlene and Gabriela fixed their silent gazes out the window and let in the magnitude of their summer.

Their bodies had tanned, become stronger, and their minds were clear as they entered the cacophony of Bucharest. At the airport, Marlene tried to check in, only to find that their flight had been canceled. She had learned basic Romanian over the summer, and with an ease that she did not recognize in herself, she conversed with the ticket agent and tried to figure out what to do next. Gabriela looked beyond at the craziness of the airport crowd.

Her eyesight was good, better than most, the doctor had once told her mother. At the far end of the terminal, there was a woman running, a woman with a violin. From a distance, it looked like she was late for a plane.

"Mom," Gabriela signed. Her mother was standing, waiting for the clerk to return.

"What, sweetie?"

"I just saw the woman with the violin!"

"What woman with the violin?" Marlene appeared distracted, annoyed at the predicament she was in.

"The same woman I saw in Berkeley, in the bathroom at the Cheese Board pizza place. Do you remember I said maybe we would see her again?"

Marlene smiled at the airline clerk, who had returned and issued them new tickets. They had been rebooks on another flight that was departing in twenty minutes.

"*Mai bine fugi!*" The airline clerk motioned with her hands that the two had better run quickly.

By the time they plopped into their seats and buckled their seatbelts, huffing and puffing, they were the last ones on the plane. Marlene looked at her daughter, took a breath, and laughed.

"Now what did you say, darling, about pizza?"

PART THREE

La Vieillesse (Almost)

Five years later

June 2000

<h1 style="text-align:center">CHAPTER TWENTY-NINE</h1>

Thérèse brushed back her graying hair. Wisps of silver outlined the reds and browns that she had the hairdresser put in each month. She looked in the mirror that morning. She saw the years fold around her face. Moments of pain and ebullience swirled over her brow, dipping into her cheekbones, folding around her chin. Everything was there in her face, she felt, as she clasped the barrette onto the soft strands of her hair, her finishing touch as she readied herself for this grand day.

She slipped on her heels and her light sweater, slung her purse over her shoulder, and closed and locked the door to her well-worn cottage. She smelled the new jasmine blossoms that had just opened the day before as she walked to her car, and as she drove into Grenoble, on that familiar highway that had been her link to the world for so many years, she opened her windows and smelled the fresh breeze. Gone were all the fields of buttercups and wild onion that would have been in full blossom at this time of year, whites and yellows that blended a cacophony of brilliance. Now, condominiums and strip malls filled those spaces. Concrete splayed out in all directions. Some would call it a brave new world. To her, it was a sign of impotence.

She parked her car in the new five-level parking garage in Grenoble. Her train was waiting, the TGV to Paris. It would get her there in a mere three hours. The train slid out of the station

147

like a woman disrobing, her silken slip falling effortlessly to the floor. As Grenoble gradually vanished from the landscape, the sprawling suburban blur finally gone, her mind then quieted as she closed her eyes for a moment.

When she opened them, the countryside beckoned her, allowing her life to unravel before her, a kaleidoscope of memories that unfolded like a fan, one image after another.

Two hundred instruments today.

Her mind lay still on that thought.

There would be two hundred instruments in Paris this evening, all being played in one room.

She had found each of those instruments, and hundreds more. For every instrument that belonged to the offspring of Holocaust survivors, she had discovered dozens of instruments whose owners were either unknown or who had no connection with the Holocaust. Her life had been this, this search, this quest, and still there were more.

Thousands more, she thought.

Two hundred was but a drop in a bucket. Yet her mind returned to those two hundred: each violin, each cello, each viola, and even the string bass that she'd found, had something in them that felt greater than life, as if there was a spirit inside each piece of wood that had died and then had become resurrected in the discovery. Holding each instrument, she somehow heard the cries, the wails, the incessant grief, the bodies thrown together, the long-ago corpses whose ashes floated like maimed fireflies in the night sky. She knew that for each of these corpses, there was music that had once been played, an angelic voice that had emerged from the bow and the instrument.

It was the soul of the instrument that she wanted to find, to uncover, to bring back to each family, so that that even just one person could put their fingers on the fingerboard and let the bow sail to the greatest depths of what it means to survive. From this fifteen-year quest that was far from over, Thérèse learned about the transcendence of music. She learned how stringed instruments resonate with the good side of humanity, the age of the wood corresponding to the wisdom and integrity that can result from the human existence, the beauty of the sound that only gets richer with age. She had learned what her mother wanted for her, yet she had learned so much more. With each instrument that she had uncovered in places all over Europe, Australia, New Zealand, Canada, and the United States, she had found a certain grandeur, a greatness, and not just in the value of these instruments, even though most of them were worth quite a bit. Rather, the grandeur inhered in the fact that at one time, before the war, all these instruments had been well loved, like beloved children, precious beings that had been born from adoring parents.

And each time she had taken the familiar train back to Paris, a new instrument in her hand, there would be, in that city where miracles happen, a reuniting of that instrument with its owner, a hosting of tears and memories that would flood the room, as family members wept and grieved, as they embraced her and Monsieur Bernovitch—the man who had created this journey for each of them.

Jakub had been approached by several other potential interns who wanted to help, and each time he resisted all their pleas. He did allow the interns to categorize and organize the instruments whose owners were unknown. There were hundreds of stringed instruments now stored carefully in a room in the building where his office was housed. First, he had told Thérèse that he thought he would auction off these instruments. Then, in a recent discussion, he revealed that his plans had changed as he readied himself to donate all those instruments to those around the world in need of music.

Over the years, he continued to let Thérèse know that he only wanted her to go get the instruments, to do the monumental work, to make the discovery. On several occasions, he reminded her that she had an innate gift for music.

"You have, my dear Madame Aguillon, an infinite understanding of the grief, the loss, and the tragedy behind each of the lost lives that our instruments represent," he had said during one of her trips to Paris. "I am certain that my vision, my dream of finding all those hidden instruments can only be actualized with your help, with your insights, your compassion, your perseverance, and your love of music. And while you are not a musician, I feel that in your soul, you are deeply musical." He paused. "And while you are not Jewish, you understand the Holocaust and what it meant to humanity."

Thérèse was quiet, not sure how to respond to all those accolades. She felt something in herself like pride, but also discomfort in expressing it, and instead changed the subject.

"I have a question for you."

"Yes?"

"Do you remember when I was about to fly to Bucharest, and you said you had a story to tell me? I was curious how you found out about the violin that turned out to be Ceausescu's Lady Blunt Stradivarius...since you never actually spoke with the couple that owned the thrift shop."

Jakub was quiet and stared out the window.

"Yes, you are a superb sleuth. You remember details. Things said and things not said." He smiled.

Thérèse looked at him, waiting for his response. For some time, she had been wondering about some of his secrets.

"I must admit, I have been withholding some information from you."

Thérèse was silent and stared at him. She saw his face turn

bright red. He was shaking.

"Are you okay?"

He paused. It appeared he was about to cry.

"Yes. This is hard to tell you."

Thérèse waited. She had been trained to wait for revelations.

"You must maintain confidentiality about what I am about to tell you."

"Of course. This is my trade."

"Yes. Of course."

He paused. Then he took a deep breath.

"I have a lover." He paused again. "She sees and hears things when I do not." He paused again. "I have not found all these instruments alone. She was the one who paved the way for you in Bucharest." Again, he paused. He seemed almost breathless. "I have known her since childhood… before the camps. She is married. Oh God, this is enough to tell you."

"It's okay. I understand. You don't need to tell me anymore. It's good you have help. It's beautiful that you love another." She was going to apologize for asking but refrained.

The subject never again came up.

* * *

Two hundred of these instruments in one room.

Thérèse stared out at the farm fields, as she fixed her mind on the project that the organization had worked on for two years. She remembered vividly the day the event was germinated.

"What if we got all the found instruments in one room?" Jakub had asked aloud that day, fingering his long beard, taking his well-worn, aged fingers, and pushing them through his wiry locks.

"What if?" Philippe had echoed, as he unwound the bow hairs of the string bass that had been discovered in Prague, brought in by Thérèse just that morning. He had remarked that the sound of the instrument was ethereal, having a quality to it that surpassed any string bass he had ever played. It had spoken to the earth, he said, this instrument in all its hugeness, its tonal depth that seemed to go beyond human consciousness.

"Yes, what if," he continued, "we invite all the owners, the families of these spectacular instruments and we have them play together in a concert, a concert that honors the survivors, an homage to those who have perished."

Thérèse and Philippe stared at Jakub and waited for him to continue.

"Yes, what if…." He paused then, thinking, his fingers pressing even more ardently into his beard, as if the thinking brain was intimately connected to the hairs growing from his face.

"These instruments mean so much to these families, to our culture, to our inner knowledge that survival of torture means everything to us as a people. In that room, on that day, as children and grandchildren and nieces and nephews of those who were gassed, in that room, music will be played, and the sounds of the ancestors, the tones of the depths of those instruments will be joined." His face turned red then, as tears welled up in his eyes.

"Brilliant," Thérèse stated simply, feeling the strength and the depth of this moment, this idea.

Philippe nodded his head in agreement. "Let's do it."

As Thérèse got closer and closer to Paris, she felt giddiness in her stomach. All those months of preparing and organizing this event were finally coming to fruition. She closed her eyes, feeling lulled by the cows outside, the miles and miles of farmland, still untainted by urban development. In that moment, the memories of all her trips to thrift shops around the world became in her mind one big blur.

But before sleep came to her, a light emerged, the little girl in the thrift shop in Carrickalinga, South Australia, Thérèse's awkward English, the child's fascination with a violin, her stare.

"Do you play the violin?" she had asked Thérèse. Her dark Aboriginal skin glowed in the sunlight that poured through the windows in the tiny shop.

"No," she answered, her voice a mixture of fact and wistfulness. "I'm getting this for a friend."

"*You* should play the violin," she said matter-of-factly. "My mama said I can play the violin one day when we get the settlement money. She said she will buy me a violin from this op shop."

"Well, then, I hope that happens soon. You sound as if you really want to play the violin."

The girl beamed and then returned to her mother, who was looking at underwear and socks. She paid for them, and the two left the store.

When Thérèse had finalized the purchase for the instrument, she stood outside, feeling the heat of the 115-degree summer day. She looked for the girl. She had disappeared. When she had arrived at the shop, she knew there was not a car except for hers outside, so she imagined the child and her mother were on foot, walking in the heat. The image of that child's face, the smile on it, a child who had a dream of playing a violin—that image played out again and again in Thérèse's mind over the years.

The violin that she had held in her hand that day, it turned out, was a Stradivarius. Ten years later, exactly five hours after the time Thérèse fell asleep on the train, she would hear that instrument again, played by Louise Loz from South Australia, the granddaughter of Jacob Loz, former first violinist with the Prague Symphony Orchestra, gassed in Auschwitz in 1942.

* * *

Thérèse sat in her seat, mesmerized by the glorious Sainte-Chapelle. For two years they had worked to secure this venue.

Gothic arches stretched out for an infinity, juxtaposing darkness and light. Color infused all, coming through the stained-glass windows and extending to the dazzling royal blue of the ceiling. The acoustics in the church surpassed any venue in all of Paris. The archbishop had, for a long time, refused their request on the grounds that there would be too many musicians and the church could not hold that number.

Jakub had done extensive research regarding the concerts that had been played there over the years. He discovered that there had been, on a few occasions, events that housed just as many musicians and singers, if not more, than the number he had proposed. He suspected anti-Semitism was the cause for the initial refusal of the permit. Bribery became the modus operandi. He offered the archbishop a fine sum. At the last minute, the church had granted them a permit.

Backstage, earlier, Thérèse had helped the musicians ground themselves. Many of them were crying, wailing even, as they pulled out their instruments and tightened their bows. Some had crossed the earth to play in this concert, and some had just taken the Métro to 4, Boulevard du Palais in the 8th arrondissement. Each musician had a story, a history of decimation, and each musician had, in their hands, an instrument found in some dusty thrift shop somewhere in the world. They came up to Thérèse, some of them never having met her, and embraced her.

Then came the call to collectively emerge into the nave of the church.

One by one, in a perfectly manicured line, they walked, violins and violas tucked under arms, cellos and one bass held as if they were children. The audience, hundreds of people seated inside and hundreds more lined up and down the streets, watching on cameras, all stood and clapped. The applause continued for about fifteen minutes, the emotion in their hands overwhelming, overpowering.

Then, the musicians sat down; the lone bass player stood like a sentry.

Jakub turned to the audience and spoke in French, Hebrew, and English. He told his story, but mostly he briefly told the stories of many. Words mingled, and underneath, there was music. Music that could survive the tortures of history, the schisms that occur in our human race.

He then sat down, and Itzhak Perlman walked to the podium, crutches in hand. The audience gasped in surprise, remembering his stunning performance of John Williams's score in *Schindler's List* that moved thousands all over the globe.

Their first piece was Edward Elgar's *Elegy, Opus 58* for string orchestra, a piece that embraced the mood of loss, of the tragedy of the Jewish people, of the hope and redemption that comes from people like Oskar Schindler and Jakub Bernovitch.

No one's eyes were dry as the violins joined with the cellos and the violas and the string bass with its deep tone. The ensemble embraced all that was part of the earth, that was part of humanity, that embedded itself in the transcendence of the pathos of the human existence. The instruments, all precious, all old, created a sumptuousness in the church, as the resounding acoustics brought that music up and over, to the gothic heights and beyond. Most of Paris, it turned out, was listening to that concert. In the streets, in tiny apartments, in lush hotel rooms, and in dimly lit restaurants and cafes, not a sound was heard except for the music that came out of that church.

After Elgar's *Elegy*, they then played Maurice Ravel's *Pavane for Une Infante Défunte*, Vaughan Williams's *Fantasia on a Theme by Thomas Tallis*, and Tchaikovsky's *Serenade for Strings in C major, Opus 48*. They finished the first section with Samuel Barber's *Adagio for Strings*.

After the intermission, the tone lightened, the somberness left behind as they played Mendelssohn's *String Symphony No. 2 in D major,* Domenico Scarlatti's *Concerto for Strings No. 3 in F,* and ended with Gustav Holst's *St. Paul's Suite.*

When the concert was over, the audience appeared to not tolerate the thought of an ending. Applause and stomping moved to a full gallop as the audience rose. All over Paris, people wanted more. For twenty minutes the applause would not stop. Then, when all was finally quiet, Perlman, with permission from the orchestra, took his own violin, and he played the solo from *Schindler's List* by John Williams. As he played, the other orchestra members cradled their own instruments. Many of them were weeping. As Perlman dug up the pathos that music was intended to create, there was, in that room, a collective sigh, a release, a moment to pause and to savor each note, as lives were remembered, as the vitality of the original musician was recalled, as the families gathered, that evening in that church, and all around the city of Paris. As they played the last notes, they knew they would never forget, and the finale to that concert remained in people's hearts for the rest of their lives.

CHAPTER THIRTY

Marlene sat in the first row. Her eyes were a puddle, and the graduation had not yet begun. A few hours earlier, she had helped Gabriela into her dress, zipping it up as she quivered in front of her now grown daughter.

How did the time go by so fast, she wondered, as nervous and excited parents and grandparents surrounded her in the auditorium at the School for the Deaf. Marlene closed her eyes and blocked out the feeling of spinning leaves, a moment in life that is just too huge to fathom. Instead, memories of fifteen years began to flood her senses. The day Gabriela walked into her preschool, right after the girl had put her entire hand into the peanut butter jar, was the day, it seemed, that she knew that her daughter would be held by myriads of people who would instantly love her. She saw in her daughter an unusual gift of a certain magnetism. At their preschool, she had seen each day how communication between the children improved because of Gabriela's presence. Not only did all the children, the staff, and the parents learn ASL, but more than that, they all learned about the power of nuanced communication. She watched as people at the school began to look at faces as they talked, using their hands to express themselves. The result had been an amazingly peaceful environment where arguments over rights and territory, a typical climate in a preschool setting, diminished.

Over the years, mother and daughter had developed a silent rule: Marlene was to mostly remain in proximity to Gabriela. This interdependence lingered, so much so that when Gabriela left preschool to go to the School for the Deaf in Berkeley, and they both moved to a little rented cottage across the Bay on Rose Street, Marlene worked at the school as an aide in all her classrooms as Gabriela progressed from the first to the twelfth grade. During PE, the only time when Gabriela enjoyed being away from her mother, Marlene collaborated with the Parent Advisory Committee. She saw how much she liked connecting with other parents in the school.

Marlene never complained, never seemed to feel that her daughter assumed too much time or too much space. And it seemed that Gabriela never felt that her mother was infringing on her space, even when she progressed to adolescence. Marlene's thoughts turned to the night when each of them decided this habit should be challenged.

Gabriela's friends were having a party at the end of tenth grade. She had seemingly become a woman overnight. Her breasts were full; her hormones were flitting around everywhere. All she could talk about with her friends were the boys in the class. Marlene remembered those days of her own adolescence so long ago, where she was confused because she had no desires for boys, ever. She would watch her daughter and her school friends signing, their hands waving in the sky like the quick, graceful reach of a dancer, as their faces lit up with flames like Stravinsky's *Firebird*. Never had Marlene experienced such passion when she was that age. In fact, Marlene had never experienced such passion. While she was so proud of her daughter and the beautiful friends she had made, Marlene was a bit envious of her too. There were some days when she wanted to be her, to experience what it meant to be surrounded by people who admired her, to know what desire felt like, to understand that the world was hers for the taking.

The night of the party arrived. Earlier that week, Gabriela's friends had insisted that Marlene stay home. They were happy to have Gabriela's mother in school each day, but this was one time when they gathered around the sixteen-year-old and made a circle, blocking Marlene from their secret conversation, pleading with Gabriela to come alone to this event. That day, Gabriela came home from school and did not eat. She had not eaten all week, either. Marlene knew what was going on and her heart was torn into bits, yet she also knew that in the school of motherhood, this was one of the first lessons: how to let go of your child. She had not attended any classes in that school, and she found it blissful that she had not had to. In her mind, there was no reason to fix something that had been working so well.

That afternoon, Gabriela had studied every inch of her body in the mirror. Marlene had purposefully given her space and did not say a word when her daughter ceremoniously locked the bathroom door, something that she'd not done before. When she emerged, a few hours later, she did not recognize the child who once had stuck her entire hand and forearm in a peanut butter jar, covering her body in an oily, oozy mess. In front of her was a beauty queen, but not in the stereotypical made-up, plastered-over way. Standing in front of her with a happy, anxious look on her face was a young woman whose long, thick, silky hair flowed around her dark skin like a feather meeting the earth. The glow from her lightly made-up face made her entire being shine like a polished amber stone, once under a fallen log and now glistening in the June early evening sun.

"Wow," was all she could sign.

"Do I look okay?"

"I can't even begin to express how gorgeous you look. You are."

"Oh, stop." She paused. "Mom, I am scared."

"You know you are going to have an amazing time. These are your friends."

"I want to stay home with you."

"No, you don't."

Gabriela's friends pulled up, ready to begin their evening, taking her baby away. Gabriela gave her one quick hug as she flew off and down the steps.

The evening turned to night, and Marlene sat motionless on the sofa, unable to do anything except stare at the walls. She refused to eat or sleep. The rational part of her knew this was ridiculous, but another, louder voice told her this was just too hard.

Sometime late that night, she emerged from her glued place on the sofa and went to the bathroom, where she, too, locked the door and examined every inch of her body. She had not ever done this, especially in the last fifteen years when she hardly even paid attention to whether both eyes were functioning or not. Upon scrutinizing her face, she noticed then the wrinkles, the lines that formed around her eyes, around her cheekbones, all the way over to her ears.

She gasped aloud, "When did I grow old?"

Her gasps echoed. Her words became locked in the graying folds of her hair, the crinkles on her hands, no longer smooth and supple. Tears took over, burning her cheeks like lemon on a cut.

There was a hard knock on the door.

Quickly splashing her face with water and drying off the traces of her internal crisis, she went to the door, looked through the peephole, and saw her daughter looking like a storm had hit her, clutching the hand of a police officer who appeared to be holding her up.

She quickly opened the door as Gabriela, reeking of alcohol and vomit, moved to her mother and grabbed onto her.

"We found her in the streets, retching. A few friends were with her, but I couldn't understand them. I don't know sign language. I do know drunkenness, and none of her friends was fit to drive her, or to drive anyone. So each of them was given a private escort service home on the condition that they don't drink again without adult supervision."

"Thank you so much, Officer. I will absolutely make sure this doesn't happen again."

"Thank you, ma'am. Good night."

Marlene took off her daughter's clothes, put her child in the bath, and made her a cup of chamomile tea. That night, Gabriela held onto her mother tightly, as she had when she was three. She never spoke of that night and what happened, and Marlene knew that she did not need to. But after that night she refused to go out with any of her friends without her mother present.

Marlene was secretly delighted.

* * *

Marlene was abruptly taken out of her reverie by the sounds of pounding drums. The school's Taiko group was announcing the start of the graduation.

It was a large graduating class, the largest the school had ever seen, eighty students all told. It was a huge year for the school because it was the last time that they would be in the location they had been housed in for more than a hundred years. The site had been deemed seismically unfit, and the school would be moving to Fremont, several miles away from its comfortable Berkeley roots. Anxiety filled the air, as one by one the class of 2000 filed in, donning the blue-and-gold caps and gowns that matched the colors of the adjoining University of California.

Gabriela entered the stage. The seriousness on her face pierced Marlene, who stared at her, eyes blurred from crying. The drums continued to beat as the graduates marched in. There was a feeling of ecstasy in the room. Some audience members clapped. Mostly the audience was on their feet, waving signs and banners, their arms uncontainable.

Then they all sat down as Gabriela went to the podium with the comportment of a royal, as she readied herself for her valedictorian speech. She had been unanimously chosen by her teachers and her peers, not only for her GPA, the highest in the class, but also for her undeterred dynamism.

She began. Her hands waved in the air like a bald eagle, flying to the depths of the spirit, the sacred spirit of all that she had become.

"My fellow students, parents, friends, teachers, and administrative staff. We are gathered here today to celebrate, to honor, to pay homage to, to love and respect all those who have taught us, raised us, and inspired us to be the beautiful beings that we are. In this school we have been taught to be proud of our Deafness, we have been taught to see Deafness as a gift, we have been given the language and the tools to explore the world of Deafness, not just in our little Berkeley, but all over the world. We, in this grand space of Berkeley, the birth of the free speech movement, have been inspired to become activists in the Deaf community, giving a voice to the voiceless in our worlds and beyond.

"I would like to tell you a story. We all have our stories, and it is a gift that I can tell you mine.

"I was born in Romania, in a time when there were no services for those who had disabilities. We were abandoned by our parents and stuck in filthy orphanages, for there was, during the time of my birth, a notion in Romania that only healthy, nondisabled children would survive the despicable times that I was brought into. My earliest memories are ones of extreme hunger, loneliness, and isolation. The speaking world surrounded me, and my world was caught in the maelstrom of a complete lack of understanding of the Deaf world.

I hid under tables, not wanting to be noticed. My future seemed destined to be perpetual agonized silence. During that time, there were two sites designated in the orphanages. On one site were the children who had few or no disadvantages. Those children were given schooling, and every day they attended classes to learn to read and write and do math and science. The other site housed the children who had what the directors called severe disabilities. Those children were denied any access whatsoever to any schooling.

"I was in that latter group. If I had stayed in that orphanage, which was most likely where I was destined, I would have not received any instruction in any subject. I would have not been understood, I would not have been given any tools to communicate. In short, I probably would have either become severely emotionally disturbed or I would have died, or perhaps both.

"My story is like a fairy tale, though, and because of it, I have always loved fairy tales.

"It is like a fairy tale because one day when I was three years old, when I was so tiny that I was like a button, a very tall woman walked into the orphanage, and she took me away. But before she did that, I had this feeling when she walked in that she was my destiny, that somehow she came to save me, and I would always love her. She didn't speak to me except with her face, which was warm and reassuring, and immediately, from that first moment, she and I bonded like two beings who were meant to be attached in some kind of primitive way that would last our entire lives. When I was so little, all I knew was to hold onto her hand and feel the warmth from it, her large hand in mine, and when I did, I knew I was safe, I knew everything would be fine.

"That's my mother, as all of you know, the one who saved my life, who gave me all the space I needed, yet stayed close because that is what we chose on that first day when she whisked me away from that despicable place to the glorious one that I am in now.

"I have thrived because of her, because of this school, because of all of you who have supported me, taught me, given me lessons on life. I have thrived because of the beauty that we see in each other, every single day, by the confidence we have given to each other to succeed, to seize the world in our talons, never backing down from adversity, from each challenge we face.

WE ARE THE CLASS OF 2000!"

Gabriela paused after this statement, stopping for the stomps, the shouts, and the cries, a cacophony of sounds emanating ebullience from every angle.

"We…." She could not continue as the stomping continued. Her face lit up with a magnanimous smile.

"We…" She paused again as the stomps reveled around her.

"We never thought we'd make it. They predicted that in Y2K, that ridiculous, ominous slaying of our minds, we would all be doomed or dead.

"Not only have we survived, but we are thriving!"

Again, she paused, as feet stomped, one by one, as boots and heels clacked on the floor, sending vibrations that echoed around the auditorium.

"We are…the new millennials, the very first ones!"

Stomps continued, the energy fierce and proud.

"I have done quite a bit of research on us, on the millennium that our generation is embarking on. Technology will be our guide. We will see, in the very near future, a combustion of new technology that not only will assist us in absolutely everything that we Deaf people need to survive and thrive, but also, most importantly, will bring us all together on this crazy yet magnificent planet we live on. We will be able to connect with others all over the world with just tiny things in our hands. The myriad of obstacles that we have faced, being Deaf, will be tales that we can tell our grandchildren about the olden days because we, as brand-new baby millennials, won't even have to go there anymore."

Stomping accelerated, the hips swayed to the rhythm as heads nodded, as the energy intensified.

"We are at the forefront, my fellow graduates, of a time in our lives where anything is possible. We will see Black men and Native Americans and Hispanics and Asians become presidents and leaders of this country; we will see women become presidents and leaders of this country, gay people become presidents and leaders of this country, socialists become presidents and leaders of this country, and yes, we will see disabled and Deaf people become presidents and leaders of this country."

Gabriela beamed at this last statement as the joyous hordes massed around her, the energy unstoppable.

"We have felt love from this school, we have felt it in all the corners, from every grade, from our wonderful teachers to the principals, from our parents even when, maybe, they didn't understand what we were going through, what it means to be Deaf in a hearing world.

"As we all go forth, we all know that we have been a fortress for each other, a knowledge that we can take with us in all places. As we all go forth, we all know that we have loved each other deeply, and with this love, we all know that we are the radiant souls on this earth. So, take that radiance, dearly beloved students, and fly like the eagles we are meant to be. Be those millennials that we are, with hope and love and with that infinite promise of change, knowing all the time that absolutely anything is possible."

With that last pronouncement, the stage erupted in noise, the feet pounced and stamped, the drums pounded, the students danced around each other, hooting like owls and eagles, eternally empowered. They took Gabriela by the hand, and all eighty students made a circle around her as still the drums wailed, and their hands waved in the air, flying.

Gabriela was radiant, her face aglow as her fellow students celebrated her words, her love. Then all was quiet as diplomas were handed out.

When commencement was over, the jubilation continued into the night, as the parents and the students partied together, as Marlene looked on proudly at her daughter, her beloved daughter, the one she'd rescued, who had also rescued her.

* * *

Gabriela didn't know where that speech would go. When she was in the middle of delivering it, she was lost in the vibrations of sound that emanated around her. Sensations blurred through her mind, her young yet packed life that swirled around her. Yet, like a gymnast, a Nadia Comăneci, she did not once let her flailing mind set her off course. She focused all her energies on the moment, on the perfection of it, on the one fact that this moment could and would affect eighty lives, eighty beings, her friends, who hung onto every one of her words and would remember this speech for the rest of their lives.

She had practiced that speech, over and over, in her living room, every night for weeks.

"I can't do it!" she would cry, her hands waving in desperate pleas in front of her mother.

"Yes, you can. Of course, you can. Just look at this as one more thing that is not easy to do but that you can do. Shall we make a list of all the obstacles and challenging things you have done in your huge life so far?" Marlene waved her hands back, her signing so perfect now after all those years of communicating with her daughter and with all her friends.

Gabriela started to laugh, finding comedy in her melodramatic life.

"No, Mom. Please don't start."

"Okay, then, just tell yourself that this is hard, but you can do it. Your classmates and all the teachers picked YOU for a reason.

166

They believe in you. And they trust and honor you."

Gabriela left the living room. Her hands were tired. She stared out the window in what had originally been her bedroom, but that had been turned into a study. Her thick, dark hair swirled around her face and covered her eyes, as she focused on the script she had written that glared at her from the computer screen.

Her mind could not focus, and instead, she pulled up the email from the Sorbonne, a letter she and her mother had received just the day before.

"Dear Madame and Mademoiselle Robinson,

We, the admitting committee at Paris-IV, Paris-Sorbonne University, are thoroughly delighted to be admitting you, mother and daughter, to our newly inaugurated International Sign Language Bachelor's Degree Program. The first term will begin in the autumn of 2000. We have never, in the long history of this University, admitted a mother-daughter team to our incoming class, and we at the Department of Arts, Letters, and Languages, are most welcoming.

Please accept our modest scholarship, with details described in a forthcoming letter provided by our finance department.

With kindest and warmest regards,

Madame Anne Hupert, Coordinator of Admissions
Paris-IV, Paris-Sorbonne

Gabriela stared again at the letter, the hundredth time she had read it since it arrived in her email box. She could not believe she was going with her mother to Paris, and together, they would be students, studying together, living together, being in Paris.

Ahhh, to be in Paris! Her feet tapped on the floor, a dance she had just invented, as she moved to the living room and danced around her mother. She then practiced her speech one last time, and at the end, she finally signed, "Okay. I'm ready."

CHAPTER THIRTY-ONE

In the first week of September, Paris comes alive again after a month of a sleepy dormancy in which Parisians close their shops and businesses and vanish, leaving behind the vast array of obnoxious tourists who take over the city.

Thérèse, like her compatriots, took a monthlong holiday from work in August, during which she slept and ate and made regular treks in the Alps, familiarizing herself with those mountains that she had always called home. She did not feel tempted to travel, however. She was always on trains and planes, finding instruments, and here was a month where she had no desire to go anywhere except her own backyard.

She loved the feeling of climbing mountains, the thin air filling her lungs. She adored watching the vast array of late-summer wild-flowers that grabbed onto the fleeting sun while the bees hovered around. There was a tiny village near her that seemed isolated in its height above sea level, and in the middle of that village there was an eighteenth-century stone church that had survived almost three hundred years of brutal mountain storms in the winters. She loved to look at this church from the outside with its mountain-ous majesty, and then venture inside and feel the age and the permanence of life, unfettered. There was a timelessness to the church. The silence beckoned her to sit still, to wonder at the awe of life, the sounds of quiet that permeated all. She thought of her mother and her sister; the silence beckoned her to remember them.

And then she would exit the church, reminded that this yearly late August ritual was an imperative part of her existence. She let the setting sun be a beacon for her long descent toward home.

As she emerged from the church, her mind felt clear as she gazed at the fullness of the mountains around her. Marlene's image came in front of her. It had been months since this happened. Her mind had been full, extremely full of the happenings in Paris, the concert, the aftermath.

And when Marlene did come to her mind, it was always the same vision: the open arms, the warm, inviting smile, the interruption in her busy life, telling her to stop, to pause and to be held. Thérèse felt swept away this time by this feeling, this interruption as she prepared to make her descent, as the sun dipped lower in the sky.

With each footstep, each path that wound itself down, away from the isolated village to other tiny villages, down through thickly wooded forests, down across the remnants of once-raging streams that were now, at the end of summer, barely trickles from the earth's surface, down to paths that led into the outskirts of the larger town, and still down to where her car was parked, there was, with each of those steps, the image of Marlene. She propelled her somehow forward. When Thérèse put the key in the ignition and started the car on the road that was now absent of all light, she felt in her a promising glow, an entrance into something she could not put a finger on. She knew, somehow, that it would change her life, that it would radically alter the older woman she was becoming.

* * *

The summer Saturday market in Saint-Ismier was, at best, a sweet slice of the delicacies of life. What used to be, several years ago, one or two stands of local farmers who sold anything from pungent sheep cheese to round and bulbous heads of garlic, was now a market hosting upwards of three dozen stands that mixed the raucous jumble of the old farmers who still sold their fragrant cheeses with the new farmers who peddled only biodynamic heads of kale and lettuce. There were also stands of this and that, locals who sold anything they could find in their homes to earn a few euros for the week.

Over the years, Saint-Ismier had been transformed in convoluted and confusing ways. In former times, it was a sleepy foot-of-the-mountain village. Now, it had turned into a town that had lost its identity in the folds of the mass development that circled around it, squeezing away its intimate vitality. The current population consisted of a hodgepodge of old-timers who did not care, who still did what they used to do, and newcomers who cared too much, whose attention was focused on making the town more pretentious. The interesting thing was that when all the development was taking place in the 1990s, no one had bothered to ask the people of Saint-Ismier what they thought about the idea.

Still, whenever she could, Thérèse enjoyed going to the Saturday market, especially when she did not want to drive all the way to Meylan or even Grenoble, where of course the markets were profuse in color, choice, and voluminous sound.

The forecast was for rain the day after her mountain hike—September 1, the last weekend before the masses returned to life in all its everyday forms. She walked to town on roads that wound about—roads that, years after their creation, still maintained their integrity. Somehow the developers had not touched her neighborhood; she hoped they never would.

It used to be that she would recognize everyone in town, and they her. Now, she only recognized a few individuals. Everyone else seemed generic, and she tended to stay away from these nondescript souls. She bantered with some of the farmers to whom she had given so much of her business over the years. When she was done shopping, her cart was full of apples and pears, cheese, late-season plums, and a host of carrots, onions, lettuce, broccoli, cauliflower, and summer squash. Her last stop was the boulangerie. She loved their brioche and their *pain complet.*

As she headed to the bakery, for the heck of it she decided to quickly peruse the nonfood stalls, something she rarely did, as she seldom needed anything that the locals brought out from their dusty homes. The last stall before the bakery was a mishmash of what seemed to be moldy and well-used or well-neglected pieces of junk. She smiled at the vendor, whom she did not recognize, and as she turned to walk away, in the corner of her eye, she spotted something that at first appeared to be a dirty, well-stained blanket. She looked more carefully and noticed, underneath the piece of fabric that hosted an array of faded colors, a violin case.

She gulped.

"Excuse me, Madame, but is that a violin?" she asked. Her voice wavered. In her mind, every violin now that was hidden away in the dusty confines of oblivion was most probably a prized possession, part of a family destroyed in despicable times.

"Yes, of course," the woman answered.

"May I look at it, please?"

"Certainly." She unzipped the case for Thérèse and pulled out the violin. "It's never been used," she said, proudly, as if this was a selling factor. Thérèse stifled her disgust. She did her usual violin-inspecting routine in which she feigned not knowing anything about the instrument and recited her standard line, "I am looking at this for a friend."

"My husband has had this instrument since he was a little boy. He said no one in the family ever played it. He didn't think it was worth anything, and he told me today to go ahead and get rid of the damn thing." She laughed.

Thérèse laughed too, more to continue the good mood to get the woman to talk more. She was seething inside.

"He had this violin since he was a little boy?" she asked, smiling, trying to be as friendly as was humanely possible.

"Yes, he was in Paris. It was during the war. Apparently, in the space of just a few months, in the better part of town, there were these fancy apartments being sold at dirt cheap prices, and my husband's parents grabbed one of these apartments. He remembered that there was this violin in the closet, which he thought strange, and he always wondered why the previous owners had not taken their violin with them. No one in the family ever wanted to play it. They were all into drums and things that make noise, and he always joked that the scratchiness of a violin is just like a piece of a big old turd after a too-heavy meal." She laughed at her joke.

Thérèse felt like she was going to vomit and tried as hard as could to emit something that sounded like a titter.

"Do you remember which neighborhood he moved to?"

"Nah, Paris is Paris, some busy neighborhood. All I know was that it was rather posh, he said." She then whispered in Thérèse's ear, "I think he said that the neighbors told his parents that once there used to be some ugly Jews there, with dirty children whose diapers were never changed."

All Thérèse wanted to do at that moment was to get that violin in her hands, get home, drop her stuff off, get in her car to the train station, and get herself to Paris. It was still early, around 10 a.m. She could do it.

"My friend would love this. It's her birthday coming up. She told me the other day she wanted a violin. What a coincidence!"

She opened her wallet. "All I have is two hundred euros. Will that suffice?"

"Yeah, that will do. My hubby will be so happy when I come

home without that old piece of wood. Got to make the old hubby happy, don't we?"

Thérèse felt vomit collecting in her throat as she handed the woman the money. She forgot about the bread, and with the violin under her arm and her other groceries in her backpack, she raced up the hill to where she could breathe again. Finally, she arrived at her front door.

Picking up the phone, breathless, she rang Paris.

"I have a new violin; I have to leave now to catch the train; I'll see you later this afternoon."

She hung up the phone quickly, not waiting to hear Jakub's response.

* * *

"Vel' d'Hiv?" Thérèse asked, knowing about the roundups on July 16–17, 1942, the Nazi-directed roundups of thousands of Parisian Jews, sent en masse to the Vélodrome d'Hiver, after which they were pushed into trains to Auschwitz. It was a hidden fact that many, if not most, of the homes these Jewish families were living in were confiscated after their departure, emptied out, and sold quickly at ridiculously low prices to French people who had no idea what had happened. No one seemed to question why or what or how, but it was the middle of the war, and money spoke louder than morals.

"Yes, sadly, most likely from the story you just told, yes." Jakub looked in her face, his own face long and solemn. Thérèse knew that he had been to the Vélodrome. He had been pushed into a train to Auschwitz, his home given away.

Just then, Philippe opened the door and greeted the two, immediately going over to the violin and picking it up.

"Wow. You've got a beauty here."

He picked it up and played a simple scale. The sound was sweet, gentle, like a cat purring on a sunny windowsill, with a soft breeze effusing a kind of elegance.

He peered inside the instrument.

"Oh my God."

He inspected the inside, peering in with his specialized scopes.

"This is the Carrodus Guarneri, one of the finest violins ever made, played by Paganini himself. Apparently, he never liked it because the sound was too soft for his flamboyant tastes and sold it during his lifetime."

Jakub walked over to his "Bible," his sacred book of records.

"This violin was owned by Schlomo Rubenstein, principal violin in the Quatuor du Printemps string quartet, which he founded. His place of residence was 686, rue de Turennes, the home that was stolen from him in 1942 and given to your despicable neighbor, Thérèse."

He went to his second book and touched the worn pages with affection.

"His granddaughter lives just around the corner. There is a note here that says she is desperate to find this instrument that belonged to her grandfather."

Breaths were all held in tightly, and there was a resonating silence in the room as Jakub picked up the phone and dialed.

CHAPTER THIRTY-TWO

"I know it was around here somewhere," Marlene signed, as Gabriela laughed.

"Mom, that's what you said a half hour ago! There are so many cafés. This is Paris, Mom, and we look like some crazed Americans with our Lonely Planet guidebook. Look, here's one. Oh my God, will you look at those strudels? We've got to go in."

She grabbed her mother by the hand, and as they opened the door to Eastern Europe, the scent of fresh pastries and the Old World wafted through their noses. They were both giddy with delight.

Marlene closed her eyes for a second, taking it all in. The sounds, the smells, the lace of life flitted around her in seductive breezes. She was in the Marais again, in Paris, and everything was coming back to her. Paris had been her lover once. She remembered how someone once told her a lover once is a lover forever.

Her mind drifted to just that morning. Gabriela was fast asleep; jet lag had consumed her. Marlene had written her a note: "I'm going out. Will return by noon. Wait for me." She slipped out into the streets, walking and walking, taking it all in. She felt something stir inside her, but she was not exactly sure what it was, and when she arrived at the Eiffel Tower, it hit her, the mass of steel—straight lines and angled ones, like lace and feathers, yet not. There were surprisingly few people there, but it was early, quite early in the

175

morning, a Sunday morning, when church bells rang for all who would listen, when smells were just beginning to awaken the senses, when Paris was just waking up, stretching out her limbs like the fine seductress she has always been, her nakedness exposed to all who gazed.

Marlene took a deep breath, inhaling the aliveness of her surroundings, feeling the pull to reveal her most precious layers that had been bound for all those years since her youth. She undid her hair and let the thickness unveil itself around her as she remembered. Memories of her first time in Paris aligned again with the essence of who she was, her own vulnerabilities, as she experienced an unleashing of her most primitive self. She walked for hours until her watch told her it was time to get back to her daughter. She then ran back to the hotel.

"Mom?" Gabriela looked over at her mom, who was out of breath and still caught in her reverie. She handed her mother a coffee and three different kinds of strudels.

Marlene bit into each one and let the sugar coat her lips. Each bite seemed irresistible. Her senses came alive for the first time in fifteen years.

"Mom, you look different. You look so…happy, you look like you are somewhere else, somewhere quite beautiful."

"Mmmm… How do I describe this? I have never talked to you about Paris, fifteen years ago…"

"You were in Paris fifteen years ago?"

"Mm-hmm. It was right before I decided to adopt you. In fact, the café I was looking for was the place I firmly made that decision."

"Really? Well, then, we should find it later."

"Yes, we should."

"But tell me, Mom, why does it feel like you are in a very special world here?"

"I was young, silly maybe, but there is something extremely wonderful about this city. More than anyone can ever tell you, and being back here, after all this time, it brings it all back. You'll see. I don't want to tell you my experiences, as I don't want to influence yours and the newness for you. Paris is to be discovered, bit by bit, neighborhood by neighborhood, café by café, museum by museum, pastry after pastry. Paris is more than a city, it is a study of the arts, of the nuances of life, the vulnerability of the soul. You'll see."

"I'll need you to get by. No one signs here."

"I'll be here with you. You know that. But there is so much of Paris that is to be seen, to be experienced without the spoken word. We will meet Deaf people here, and we will be able to perfect our French signing, and we will make friends here. But the most important thing is just to let it all in, this truly magical city." Marlene's eyes were misty as she felt herself brought back to a story, her own fairy tale that she had put on pause so many years earlier. She listened to the French voices around her. This time, she understood what they were saying. There were two older women complaining about their husbands. She laughed.

"I understand French now. Those two women are complaining about their two-bit husbands. When I was here before, I didn't understand a word of French."

"Le Camp des Loups."

"Absolutely. Here's to Le Camp des Loups!" They clinked their coffee cups.

Every summer since Gabriela was four, the two of them had gone to Île d'Orléans in Québec for Deaf summer camp, the Camp of the Wolves. They looked forward to being there every year because the ambience was friendly and warm. While most of the kids and families came from Québec, there were some, like themselves, who came from all over the United States and Canada.

Signing was in ASL and LSQ (Langue des Signes du Québec), and the speaking parents conversed mostly in French, with some English thrown in.

"I never thought that French would sink in like that. You'll find that's true, I'm sure, when we find another Deaf person to speak with."

"Mom, there's one right behind you."

Marlene turned around, and Gabriela signed, "Hi."

Camera wrapped around his neck, the man did not respond to Gabriela, as he was peering at his green Michelin book. His wife spoke in a loud voice to what appeared to be her daughter next to her. Their voluminous, piercing American accents made Marlene cringe, especially as they were bickering about the cost of things in Paris. The children spoke only in English, and the Deaf father signed to his wife. The children ignored the dad. *Strange,* Marlene thought.

Still, politeness took precedence, and Marlene tried as well. She signed "Hi" and then said "Hi." They looked up. The father nodded glumly and then returned to his book, and the mother yelled out, "Ah, another American. How great is that! Can you believe these prices here? I mean you can get pastries for much, much less at Costco. I wonder if they have Costco here in Paris. I should check it out."

"I am not sure. Well, do enjoy your stay here." She got up to leave, and Gabriela, appearing to have understood exactly what was going on, quickly followed.

When they were out of sight and earshot, they started to laugh.

"Please don't tell me that we are like that, the stupid Americans that have no clue. The dysfunctional family in Paris."

"No, of course not. We do have a better sense about us, of course we do," Marlene laughed. "She was asking if Paris has a Costco."

"Is that what it was? Okay, do we need to spend time thinking about the stupid things that people say?"

"Only if we want to write a comedy."

"Seems more like a tragedy to me."

"Yeah, you're right."

"Hey, Mom, look at the size of those challahs!"

"They're gorgeous. Let's get one."

As they walked into the bakery, the freshly baked hamantaschen met the challahs with an aroma of yeast, poppy seeds, eggs, jam, and the feeling that life had stopped for pleasure alone. Nothing of wars and exterminations could be sensed at that moment, when the sweetness of all that was good in humanity came to them as they stood, waiting their turn, watching the Hasidic customers converse with the shop owner.

They walked out with a bag bulging with an assortment of breads and pastries. A procession blocked the street. Lining the rue de Turennes was a wedding party, women dressed in vibrantly colored silks and linens, high heels clicking a rhythm on the pavement. The men, on the other side of the street, were all in long black coats and high hats, with white shirts and tzitzits, their rope knots hanging loosely from their trousers. The violins and the accordions played in a minor key, as the clapping sounds echoed off the old stone walls. Then came the bride and groom, the white of her dress dazzling in the late afternoon sun. The inlaid pearls, embraced in silk, were luminescent jewels that highlighted the delicate curves of her body. She held the hand of her husband; their smiles lit up the street.

And then, as if this were a sweet mirage, the procession moved down the street, to an area that was blocked off, as the bride and groom disappeared into a building that had survived all the wars. The party followed as normalcy resumed its regular pace on the street.

"Wow!" was all Gabriela could sign.

"This is Paris," was all Marlene could sign back.

The packed Sunday streets had a flow, a direction, and Marlene and Gabriela followed it, as if there was a force in that city that led one to places of magic and destiny.

"Here it is," Marlene said, simply.

"The café you were looking for?"

"Yep."

They walked in. It was as busy as she remembered from fifteen years earlier. Immediately, Marlene felt a tug at her heart, something she could not put her finger on, as she asked the waiter if they could sit at the same table where she'd sat so long ago. She faced the door and placed her chair at the same angle that she remembered, looking out. Gabriela wanted to look out too, to see Paris as well, and thus they sat side by side.

"*Bonjour, Madame, Mademoiselle. Quelque chose à boire?*" Something to drink?

"*Est-ce qu'on pourra regarder le menu, s'il vous plaît?*"

"*Bien sûr.*" He handed each of them a menu of beverages and food.

"Very nice, Mom."

They both laughed.

Marlene fixed her eyes on the menu, trying to decide if she was hungry or just too excited to even think about food.

"Uh, Mom…someone just walked in the door, and she is staring right at us. Um, no, she is staring right at you."

Marlene looked up.

There, standing like a statue, looking like time had never moved, like the clocks had somehow become transfixed in an immutable moment in history, Thérèse, stared at Marlene from just inside the doorway. Her eyes focused on her face, scanning it from right to left. Marlene felt this gaze through her, and she began to swoon inside. She was brought back to that infinite moment at Versailles.

With one subtle glance, Marlene beckoned Thérèse to the table. As Thérèse's footsteps moved in one slow motion toward her, Marlene felt her heart quicken, her breath no longer one indistinguishable quiet hum.

She sat down in a chair that Gabriela took from the neighboring table.

Gabriela then took out a piece of paper and a pen and wrote out, "AND WHO ARE YOU?? ACTUALLY, I HAVE SEEN YOU BEFORE. IN BERKELEY. AND THEN YOU WERE RUNNING LIKE A CRAZY WOMAN AT THE AIRPORT IN BUCHAREST." She handed it to Thérèse with a smile.

"I…"

Marlene put her hand out in a *Stop* gesture as she began to translate.

Thérèse shook her head, and with a nod of her head, she took the pen and the paper and wrote out: "My name is Thérèse. Berkeley. Let me remember. I got the violin. No, you weren't there. Then I went to the pizza place." She paused.

"The bathroom," Gabriella wrote. "You did not wash your hands. It was disgusting."

"Oh my God, *of course* that was you in the bathroom. Oh my God!! Were you the one who did a circle of salt and sugar packets around the pepper shaker? I don't why I remember this so many years later, but I do," she wrote. She paused and looked again at Gabriella. "Yes, I had a bad habit of not washing my hands. My apologies for grossing you out. I do wash my hands now… Bucharest?... What in the world were you doing there???"

Gabriela laughed.

Then, Thérèse took the pen again.

"I met your mother fifteen years ago. I am assuming that is your mother."

"Yes," she wrote back.

Gabriela signed to her mother, "I can see it all, Mom. This is sweet. I am going to go out to explore the neighborhood. I think the two of you need time to talk. I'll be back soon." She winked.

Marlene, dizzy, turned to her daughter. "Lovely. Thank you." Gabriela pranced out of the cafe, a swing in her step, a little bounce as she reached the curb outside.

Thérèse sat across the table from Marlene, her eyes fixed on the woman whose gaze was only on her.

Together they sat in silence, studying each other's faces.

Instinctively, their hands reached out and clasped, but their eyes never moved, as the heat of their skin burned, two incendiary energies colliding in that café on the rue de Turennes.

After several minutes, Marlene broke the silence, in French this time.

"I never forgot that day."

"Nor did I."

"You speak French now," Thérèse laughed.

"And you speak English now." This time they both laughed, their faces lighting up like fireflies on a summer evening.

"I can truthfully say that you've been with me during all this time. Your image, that night, kept returning to me like a reprise, a notice that I wasn't supposed to forget," Marlene said, her voice soft, delicate.

"The exact same experience happened with me. Time after time, unexpectedly I would see your face, a reminder of that night, a reminder to me that you and I would meet again." Thérèse studied Marlene's face, noting her tears. She took her fingers and lightly stroked the moisture that was flowing down Marlene's face, her gaze constant, gentle.

"You are beautiful," she said, kissing Marlene's fingers and then holding them to her cheeks.

They both sighed, as people came and went, as waiters moved swiftly by, as time stood completely still for them in that moment at the table.

"We have stories to tell. You have a daughter."

"Yes."

"We just missed each other in the bathroom that day ten years ago. If only I had washed my hands, then I would have seen you."

They both laughed then, hard, as the tears began to fall from their eyes. Their hands clasped tighter. And they told their stories, the weaving in and out of violins, and two trips to Romania, and cellos, and a Deaf daughter, and snowstorms and babies being delivered, and illegal vaccinations, and a concert, and a graduation. Their words jumbled together like autumn leaves, swirling around, their lives in motion, full and passionate, purposeful, spontaneous, and giving. Each had nourished, and each had been nourished by these lives. They saw this in each other's eyes, in the telling of their stories, this love that they had to share, this love they needed to share, this part of their existence that had held each together during those fifteen years like the blood that pulsed in their veins. Their English and French mingled together in their conversation like honey and nuts on a flourless torte.

"We are different now," Thérèse said.

"Yes. Is it old age, or is it wisdom?"

Just then, Gabriela returned.

"Tell me that last line?" she asked, giggling.

Thérèse took the pen, and wrote down, "I said, we are different now, and your mom said, 'Yes. Is it old age, or is it wisdom?'"

"I say it's both," Gabriela wrote as they all laughed.

They, all three, then walked out together, into the beginnings of the evening, the lights of Paris swirling through each of them for different reasons. Looking at Gabriela's face, one could not help but notice that she had fallen in love already with this city.

On the faces of her mother and Thérèse, there was a clarity now of destiny, of lives finally coming together, realizing in that moment that they had fallen in love with each other fifteen years ago, reminding each other that once one falls in love with another, that love never goes away. They whispered that fact to each other, kissing each other's earlobes, as Gabriela walked ahead, her eyes fixed on her future, on this city that was seducing her, tantalizing her, and calling her into its mesmerizing hold.

She turned around, smiling at her mother and Thérèse. When they came up to her, she signed, "I am drawn into this city. I must go out tonight. I must feel Paris before I sleep."

Her mother's face grew worried.

"I'll be okay. It won't be like that time in high school. Remember, Mom, when we talked about trust?"

All Marlene could do at that moment was to not hide her giggle, her memory of her own impassioned yearnings for this city. She looked at the face of her daughter, the child she had raised who was no longer a child. A young woman, filled with all the desires of her age, was reminding her about trust.

"I love you, sweetheart. Enjoy this city with all of who you are. You have the key. Let yourself in when you are ready to sleep."

Gabriela hugged Marlene and then Thérèse, skipping away, her hair bouncing around her shoulders as the warm August evening breeze floated through the air.

* * *

Thérèse and Marlene watched Gabriela dance away. Thérèse took Marlene's hand and kissed every finger, her tongue caressing each particle of skin that laced the digits. Marlene moaned quietly. Her knees became weak as Thérèse turned to her and placed her lips gently on Marlene's. She wrapped one hand around Marlene's back and pulled her closer.

The moon began to rise, huge, over the Pont des Arts, a bulbous sphere of light that reflected off the Seine.

"Let's take a taxi to the hotel," Marlene murmured, her body sinking, her moans growing more intense as Thérèse's lips pressed with insistence against hers. She felt the beginnings of starvation, wanting only this, yet also wanting so much more. "We have a few hours before Gabriela returns," she giggled.

Thérèse did not speak, but her breathing grew louder. Her body leaned into Marlene's, and her legs cradled around hers, pressing in farther.

Marlene looked up, not wanting this moment to stop yet also wanting privacy. A taxi drove by, and she hailed it, as Thérèse ran her fingers through Marlene's hair and winked at her. Within minutes, they were at the door to the hotel room. Marlene fumbled through her purse for her key as Thérèse teased her earlobes with gentle kisses.

Once inside, Thérèse's hands undid buttons, unzipped zippers, her fingertips scratched at skin, as Marlene's hands did the same. Now finally naked, they felt their lips irresistibly join like magnets, as they pulled each other to the bed. Their moans grew louder as Thérèse slid down and tasted the wetness of Marlene's body. Marlene's hands held Thérèse's head, pressing it against her. Thérèse slid her tongue inside, whereupon Marlene gasped, then panted. She grabbed at Thérèse's hair, her moans turning to screams that echoed. She then pulled Thérèse up and kissed her, and they folded around each other, cooing, caressing, calming, and holding, as the moon outside rose to its highest, a magnificent roundness in the sky, its light reflecting the energy of surrender.

CHAPTER THIRTY-THREE

Four years later

June 2004

Paris

Thérèse sat next to Lucien in the ornate nineteenth-century Grand Amphitheatre of the Sorbonne. Images of Pascal and Descartes surrounded them. Each one sported a gold engagement ring. They spoke in French.

"Tell me how you met Gabriela." Thérèse's eyes glittered. She recalled the first time she had met her, in the bathroom in Berkeley. Gabriela had unforgettable eyes; they seemed to pierce directly into a person's soul, like those of an owl.

Lucien laughed. His dark wavy hair softly met his neck and bounced when he laughed.

"I wanted to learn Romanian Sign Language." He paused and fingered his ring and smiled. His face turned red. He seemed shy, reticent to continue.

"Why would you be intrigued by Romanian Sign Language?" Thérèse was adept at momentarily changing a topic to help someone feel at ease...so eventually they could return to her first question.

"My eight-year-old niece inspired me. She is Deaf." He stopped and looked down. Thérèse nodded for him to continue. "My sister and her husband, her parents, did not want to accept her condition, which the doctors diagnosed when she was a toddler. They forced her to lip-read and integrate into regular schools in Bucharest. My brother-in-law comes from wealth, and they live in a fancy house, in a posh neighborhood with bling-bling attitudes, tutors, maids, and everything you can think of—except compassion for and acceptance of their only child's disability. Many times, I suggested that Nadia, my niece, learn sign language, and they, my sister and brother-in-law, only laughed in my face. I witness so often how she struggles with language and identity. They are forcing her to live in a world that is not hers, where she has no means to express herself through a nonwritten language. It breaks my heart. After a lot of soul-searching, I decided I want to not only learn sign language, but I want to incorporate it into a plan of study that would allow me to reach others in my home country. When I discovered the sign language degree program at the Sorbonne, I became enthused. It completely resonated."

He paused and smiled and fingered his ring. Thérèse smiled and nodded her head. She knew what was coming next.

"Do you believe in love at first sight?"

Thérèse nodded and laughed. "Yes. Absolutely!"

"When I met Gabriela in class that first day six months ago, I knew she was the woman I wanted to marry." His face became even redder.

"Her eyes?" Thérèse chuckled.

"*Oui. Tout à fait.*" He laughed. "But more than that, her essence. The way she carried herself in that room, commanding an audience with her beauty and determination. When we began to communicate, I felt the depth of her energy."

"Were you already fluent in French Sign Language?"

"Yes. Completely. I learned it quite fast. I was surprised by how quickly I learned. You know my mother is French. So, it felt like an extension of my mother tongue. Gabriela and I learned Romanian

Sign Language as if it were another extension of ourselves. You probably don't see this, but when she is communicating in her native language, an entirely different part of her comes out. It is richer and even more expressive than when she is signing in English or in French."

Thérèse nodded. "That would make total sense." She paused. "How come you two didn't meet earlier? The program isn't that large."

"You know, one would think we would have. But I am in my third year, and she is in her fourth and final. For some reason the program separates the years quite rigidly. They have a strict program of study for each level. It's good that way. One feels less intimidated." He laughed. "I had to put a little pressure on them for me to enroll in the Romanian class. It was meant for only graduating seniors, but the enrollment was low, so they let me in." He smiled, paused, and looked dreamy.

"Was it love at first sight with you and Marlene? You nodded quite enthusiastically when I asked earlier." Lucien chuckled.

"*Tout à fait.*" They both laughed at their shared common denominator. Lucien's hair again flopped around his shoulders as if it was dancing.

"Though it took us fifteen years to realize it…"

Thérèse looked as if she might cry.

* * *

Marlene and Gabriela were backstage, sweating and pacing. Three dozen other men and women were doing the same. In just a matter of moments, they would be receiving their diplomas in the Sorbonne's first graduating class in the Department of International Sign Language. Normally, departments held graduation ceremonies only for doctoral degrees, but because this was such a pivotal inaugural year, the University had waived all protocol.

In four years, each graduate had learned at least three sign languages. French and English were obligatory. The third was of each student's choice. In addition, each student had to take a host of required courses in political theory, science and technology, mathematics, social psychology, history, ethics, literature, and contemporary legal issues in Deaf studies.

In those four years, Gabriela learned that she could survive without her mother. She began the program, though, full of doubts and fears. Never had she experienced such inner torment, noticing how her sense of self began to diminish when she stepped into that first class, realizing that she was the only profoundly Deaf person in the room. She immediately acknowledged to herself that she was the only one in that sea of faces who had never heard a piece of music, the human voice, waves at the ocean, an infant's cries. In the beginning, her mother was her crutch, but shortly after the beginning, she no longer wanted her mother in this role.

"Mom," she signed one day in late September in their first year, "something is happening to me. I feel like I am losing myself."

"What do you mean?" Marlene signed back.

"Do you remember how we made a pact fifteen or so years ago that we would never separate from each other?" She did not wait for her mother to respond. She signed rapidly, "It was our game, wasn't it? But it was also real. I felt that I needed you to live. And maybe you experienced the same." Then she laughed.

Marlene laughed and smiled.

"But it worked for all those years. Hey, look at us, we even convinced the esteemed faculty at the Sorbonne, of all places, that we are a team, that we are dependent on each other, interdependent."

Marlene nodded and smiled.

"But something is changing in me, Mom. I am not quite sure what it is. I am terrified here. I am the only profoundly Deaf person in our program. And at the same time, I don't want to lean on you like I have all these years." She paused. "Is this wrong?"

"Is your last question rhetorical?" Marlene signed.

They both laughed.

"You…and I knew this was going to happen one day. Right? You are supposed to want to grow up. I knew you would decide when that would be."

"Yes, but I feel like I am slipping. I am so uncomfortable with myself. I have never felt this, Mom."

"This is the first time since you were a teeny child, except for that motel horror, when you have been in a place where you are the minority. You have been surrounded by those like you for fifteen years. And every time you weren't in the majority, I was there. I knew I was part of the problem, but it was our understanding that it would be like this. It was our sweet reality. I knew, though, that one day it wouldn't be so. And I knew that would be a good thing. It's called growing up."

"But it feels so… I don't really have a word for it. Googie."

"Googie?" Marlene laughed.

"Yes, it's a word I just made up. It's like it feels yucky."

"It's like the child is fighting with the adult who wants to emerge but is not quite sure how."

"Yep." She paused. "But how am I going to communicate with everyone here?"

"Just like you always do, darling. With your whole beautiful, dynamic, and passionate self."

Gabriela began to cry and reached over to her mom and wrapped her arms around her and squeezed her tight. Then she turned and walked away. She did not see her mother cry as she watched her daughter cross that threshold.

* * *

Gabriela studied hard those four years. Not only was the quality of assignments much more challenging than what she was used to, but also her motivation to truly excel surpassed anything she had ever experienced in herself. She grew to love learning, and it helped her to move away from her childhood longings for her mother's companionship. She made many friends, and Paris was the venue for their escapades.

One year slipped to the next as she found herself, time and time again, loving her life, her choices, Paris, being an adult, being Deaf.

"Mom, Thérèse," she announced one day over Sunday lunch. This was the time in the week when she and her mother and Thérèse, if she was there, came together to talk and share. On weekday evenings and on weekends, she either studied or went out with friends. In class, she and her mother were colleagues, and while they shared information, there was a noticeable distance between them that they had agreed to uphold.

They looked up. Thérèse followed every movement of her hands. She had become very adept at the language.

"I am getting married," she said simply, her face lit up like the Eiffel Tower on the Fourteenth of July.

* * *

When Lucien walked in the classroom for the first time, just a few minutes after she had arrived and had begun to settle in, she sensed his presence before she saw him. His scent reminded her of something as he sat down next to her and introduced himself. *What is it?* she wondered. The second thing she noticed was his hair. It was positively gorgeous. Wavy down to his shoulders. Dark. So were his eyes. She decided that he was someone to stare at and not get tired of.

"Hi. I am Lucien," he signed.

"Hi. I am Gabriela." She paused. "Okay. Romanian Sign Language course. Why?"

"You cut to the chase, don't you?" He laughed. "I am half Romanian."

"Which half?"

"Dad."

"And your mom is French?"

"Oui. *Tout à fait.*" He paused. "Jewish," he added in a quieter tone.

"You?" His face lightened. He seemed content to take the focus away from this last addition.

"100 percent."

"French?"

"Nope. That's zero percent."

"Let me guess. Romanian."

"Yep."

"So why are you in a class to learn Romanian Sign Language?"

"Because I don't know it."

The professor then waved his hands and commanded silence to start the class.

Lucien shook his head and smiled. Gabriela felt excessive moisture in her hands and could barely pick up her pen to take notes. *He smells of Romania, that farm, those walls, the earth. Oh my God.*

She picked up her pen somehow and scribbled a quick note. "Go for a drink after class?" She surreptitiously passed it to him. He looked at it and smiled and nodded yes.

They talked for hours that first day, one story after another. Neither stopped smiling. Gabriela felt something in her body stir around madly, shifting and transforming everything she had known about herself.

The first day led to the second, and then to the next week and the following. Their conversation was dynamic. Neither missed a beat. Gabriela felt like she was home with this man.

They spoke the obvious from the very beginning.

"We have the beginnings of a life together, you know," Lucien signed, six weeks after they had met, a little more than three months before Gabriela's graduation.

"I knew when you first walked in the door. I smelled it. I knew you were the man I would marry."

"Let me ask you the formal way. Will you marry me, beautiful Gabriela?" He got down on one knee at a bench at Parc Monceau. Spring emerged in front of them, bright yellow daffodils bursting everywhere in the park.

"Yes, yes, and yes, Lucien, dearest Lucien."

"And this is just the beginning." Gabriela sighed as she leaned into him. The late afternoon sun wafted around them. It seemed that all of Paris applauded, asking for an encore.

* * *

"Wonderful!! Wonderful!! Wonderful!!" Marlene and Thérèse signed in unison. They were absolutely, positively ebullient.

"Get him over here right this instant!" Marlene signed. "We absolutely must toast the two of you."

Gabriela laughed as she pulled out her phone and sent Lucien a text message.

How convenient! I was just in the neighborhood. I will be right over.

Within ten minutes he was seated at the dinner table, opening a bottle of champagne.

Everyone had fallen in love with the charming, delightful, and intelligent French-Romanian the moment he was introduced to the family earlier that year. They all toasted again and again.

"Here's to love." Therese sighed and beamed as she looked from Gabriela to Lucien and watched Gabriela's entranced face, Lucien's devoted eyes.

Then Gabriela signed, "Mom, you and Thérèse should get

married too. On the same day, a joint ceremony."

They all laughed.

"No, just the two of you," Marlene responded. "You don't need us old farts."

"For one, you two are not old. And for two, it would be oh-so-marvelous to have a double love ceremony." Everyone laughed at Lucien's audaciousness.

"Why not?" Thérèse chimed in. She reached over and kissed Marlene.

They toasted again, beaming.

* * *

Lucien squirmed in the chair. Gabriela was the only one who noticed.

"Tell them." she signed.

"Tell us what?" Marlene signed back, serving the dessert, a luxurious crème brulée. She had completely mastered the art of French cooking.

Lucien, usually so confident and suave, shook a bit as he put his hands up to speak.

"My grandmother will insist we have a rabbi bless our union." He paused. "My parents won't care. My dad's not even Jewish."

Thérèse and Marlene were silent. On Thérèse's face, thoughts moved around like a storm at sea. She seemed to put one idea in front of the other as she looked intently at Lucien.

"Tell us about your grandmother," she signed. "You have never spoken of her or your Jewish origins."

"I don't talk about it much. It's just not something we do in my family. But then I realized if I get married, my grandmother will give me hell if I don't have either a Jewish wedding, or at least a blessing by the rabbi."

"Let's put aside the wedding for the moment. Do you feel okay to talk a bit about your family? Anything? A story?" All eyes were on Thérèse and Lucien. Everyone knew that when Thérèse wanted to know something, she didn't let go.

"None of us know very much, actually." He paused. "The stories were not really shared. My grandmother's father played the violin. The family was sent to the Vélodrome, then to Auschwitz, where they all perished. The night before the Vichy came and took them and my grandmother's baby sister, they hid my grandmother in a church in the next town. My great-grandparents paid the priest and told him that after the war, they would come back and get her. My grandmother was eight years old. She never saw her family again. The priest took care of her throughout the war, and when it was over, he encouraged her to get baptized. This, apparently, she did willingly. She lived a Catholic French life, married a Catholic, but then, just a few years ago, she told her family of her origins, and they encouraged her to talk to a rabbi. This, she did, and he suggested that she consider converting back to her religion of origin. She did, but it remained a secret to anyone outside the family." Lucien paused. He was still shaking a little.

"You don't tell many people this story, do you?" Thérèse asked.

Lucien shook his head.

"What happened to the violin?" Marlene nodded her head. It seemed she knew this question would eventually come up.

Lucien stared hard at Thérèse.

"Oh, my amazing God," he signed.

"What was your grandmother's last name?"

"She never told us, but one day I was in her house, and she asked me to find something in her kitchen cabinet. There was a small stack of letters that were behind her cookbooks, as if she was hiding them. They were addressed to Rahel Yitzhak. She was known to the world as Nathalie Duval." He was silent. His hands shook.

"I found your grandmother's violin. Hmmm…it was about five

or six or so years ago. I remember meeting her. I found it in a thrift shop in Berlin. It was a very valuable instrument. A Stradivarius." She paused. "Were those letters from Jakub Bernovitch?"

"Yes."

"We asked her to play in the concert in the year 2000…the one where the family members played the recovered instruments that were stolen by the Nazis. It was an extremely moving event. I imagine that's what was in the contents of the letters. Your grandmother did not attend. It must have been so hard for her."

"This was before the family knew anything." He paused. "It was strange, because one day about five years ago, she came home with a violin. It looked old. She told us she maybe wanted to play again. She said that when she was in high school, she played a bit, but then lost interest and gave away her violin. I don't think she has even touched it. The last I looked it was in her attic."

Thérèse nodded her head. "Five years ago, yes, 1999. Yes, that is when I was in Berlin. I cradled that instrument for a moment before I brought it up to Paris to show Monsieur Bernovitch. It smelled like peace if you know what I mean. It had a delicious sound, a very sweet tone. His assistant discovered that it was made in 1720 and was owned by your great-grandfather, who played in L'Orchestre National de France before the war."

Lucien sat in silence for a moment. "After she got that violin, everything seemed to change in the family. Shortly after, she talked to the rabbi and then did the conversion process. I think that violin brought her back to who she had been hiding from, even if she never said a word about it to her family."

"How did things change?"

"She seemed happier. I can't really describe it more than that."

Everyone was quiet then, joining the quiet between Thérèse and Lucien, the kind of quiet that reigns when a huge secret has finally been released, and what is left is a state of calm.

CHAPTER THIRTY-FOUR

Gabriela and Lucien stood in a verdant courtyard outside the synagogue. The reform rabbi recited a *misheberakh*, a blessing honoring their soon-to-be home filled with love. The entire procedure took five minutes.

Lucien's grandmother was the only witness. Her eyes were filled with tears. She could barely contain them.

Outside the synagogue, the rest of Lucien's family, Marlene, and Thérèse joined the grandmother and the bride and groom. They all stepped into the limousine and headed to Parc Monceau for the wedding.

It was a stunning event on the gorgeous stone steps at the park. Three wedding dresses and a tuxedo. All was silent except for the waving of hands. Even the city councilor who performed the marriage signed.

A young child with his mother, sitting on a bench near the ceremony, yelled in a loud voice, "Maman, is that man marrying the three women? And why is no one talking?"

"Shhh…no," she said in a quiet voice. "He is marrying only one of them. The other two women are marrying each other. And they *are* talking. With their hands. Just watch."

The little boy stared with amazement.

"When I grow up, I want to marry three women in beautiful dresses and wave my hands in the air like birds," he stated, a bit more quietly.

There were flowers everywhere, those blooming in the park and bouquets brought in by the guests. Accompanying the sweet smell was the aroma of freshly baked strudel that surrounded a grand three-tiered wedding cake adorned with more flowers and strawberries. Champagne bottles, ready to be opened, filled another table.

When the brief ceremony was over, the guests ate, drank, and laughed but mostly hugged the two married couples.

Standing by a tree in bloom, Monsieur Bernovitch watched the guests. He stared at one person; his eyes fixed on her face. It seemed he recognized her. Thérèse came up, her face aglow.

"Mazel tov, Thérèse. That was beyond beautiful."

She beamed. "I see you are looking at Rahel Yitzhak. She is the one who did not attend the concert. She is Lucien's grandmother."

"Oh my God." He paused. "So, it comes around. I was wondering if any of the monumental work you have done would ever touch your own family."

Thérèse nodded. She had tears in her eyes.

"No tears. It's your wedding day." He put his arm around her. "Come, let's go and talk to her."

"Do you think she wants this?"

"Yes. I believe she does."

They both approached her. She was holding a glass of champagne and talking to her daughter.

"Excuse me. I am so sorry to interrupt, Madame Duval."

"Oh, please do, Thérèse, and call me Rahel." She paused. "That was such a beautiful wedding. It made me cry. Very different kind of wedding than one expects. I am so happy for my grandson. He seems happier than I have ever seen him." She paused again. "And thank you for insisting that they have a blessing by the rabbi. That meant a lot to me."

"Of course, Rahel. It just seemed normal to do this." She paused and made a sign to Jakub to come closer.

"Rahel, I believe you met this man several years ago, in 1999. May I reintroduce him…Jakub Bernovitch." She turned to Jakub. "Monsieur Bernovitch…this is Madame Du…"

"Yitzhak, Madame Yitzhak." Rahel stared at Jakub. "You do look familiar."

Jakub held out his hand. "*Enchanté.* He paused and looked in her eyes. "My organization found your father's violin. Thérèse, to be exact, found it in Berlin."

"*Mon dieu.* That was Thérèse who found it?"

He nodded.

Rahel moved closer to Thérèse and embraced her. She began to cry. Huge tears streaked her face and fell onto Thérèse's shoulders. Then she embraced Jakub.

"That violin changed my life," she said in a quiet voice. "It gave me back my identity that I had hidden from the world—and from myself, for almost seventy years."

No one quite knew what else to say. They all let that last statement sink in with a quiet hush.

* * *

When the wedding was over and all the guests had left, the two couples sat down on the same bench where Lucien had proposed to Gabriela just a few months earlier. It was early evening, and the light was fading.

"Let's take a picture of our four wedding rings," Gabriela signed.

Everyone beamed as a passerby clicked Lucien's camera. Four hands shot up, two upon two interlocked as the jewels on each glistened in the late spring sun. Memories of the stunning day made each person feel deliriously, deliciously happy.

"Now that was a *great* idea," Marlene signed.

The others nodded their heads as the sun began to dip below the tops of the trees and the evening birds began their songs of courtship.

CHAPTER THIRTY-FIVE

Shortly after the wedding, Gabriela and Lucien managed to find a *chambre de bonne* ...a tiny room they rented on the tenth floor of a beautiful Haussmann building in the 8th arrondissement. It suited them well.

While Lucien ensconced himself in his last year of studies, Gabriela interviewed for jobs. She was in high demand, and several organizations throughout France and the rest of Europe tried to woo her. The United Nations was her first choice. They hired her, with an impressive salary, to start up a new organization to assist Romanian Deaf children. She would be teaching them sign language, helping them integrate into their communities, and allowing them to experience freedom in their own countries.

She found a beautiful apartment in Bucharest, overlooking the Danube. The newlyweds began to divide their time between Paris and Bucharest.

They both continued their Sunday lunch gatherings as often as they could with Marlene and Thérèse. Each time they toasted their lives, their new adventures, the forging of selves emerging from love. Gabriela always added, "And here's to Paris, that has brought us here, that has inspired us, and that we will never, ever leave."

They all agreed.

One Sunday, a year after the wedding, Thérèse interrupted the flow of endless signing.

"Announcement, announcement, ladies and gentleman."

Everyone laughed.

"I am finally retiring from my psychiatry practice. I have just found a buyer for my cottage in Saint-Ismier, and your mother and I have just bought a gorgeous, light filled two-bedroom flat in the 15th arrondissement, overlooking the Seine."

"Wow!!!" Lucien got up and readied himself to lift the two on their chairs.

"Wait! There's more!" Marlene signed. "L'Ecole des Myrtilles has just hired me to be their director!" Marlene had been working for the past year as a teacher at this small, sweet school for the Deaf in the heart of the Marais.

"Wow wow wow!!!" Lucien started moving furniture.

"Wait!!! There's still more!!" Gabriela beamed and stroked her belly.

"Oh my God!!" Marlene screamed.

"Yes, we are going to have a baby." Lucien was red in the face and beaming.

"Beautiful things happen in packages of three," Thérèse stated, simply, as they raised their glasses over and over.

* * *

Lucien graduated at the end of that year and joined Gabriela in her work with the organization in Romania, where they were both granted a national medal of honor. A few months later, Gabriela gave birth to a little girl that they named Manon. They raised her in a bilingual world.

Adorable little Manon fell in love with Paris as a toddler. One of her favorite things to do was amble about the grass, laughing under the Eiffel Tower, pointing her fingers upward as she stretched her neck to see the very top.

Listen to the Paris concert at the
Sainte Chapelle on Spotify!

https://open.spotify.com/playlist/3opSlanZdBOOOzpmSz7M9D

Epilogue

Marlene and Thérèse sat on a lawn by the Seine. Entwined in each other, they felt the warm summer night breezes caress their skin. They turned to each other, their lips finding fire, finding comfort, finding music, finding it again and again, as the twinkling sounds of the distant carousel, as the lights and the smells of all that was Paris surrounded them with a familiar hum. As they got up to leave, hand in hand, walking through the streets that refused to sleep, they kicked up leaves that had, like pillows, landed at their feet. They laughed, their lips joining again, as they would that night in bed, as they would for years and years, the harmony of life effortlessly caressing them.

Thérèse continued to find string instruments, collecting close to five hundred instruments in her lifetime. Marlene worked as director of the school for decades until her retirement at the age of eighty.

Manon became a regular visitor to Paris. She eventually learned to play her great-great-grandfather's violin. When she was sixteen, she performed as a busker under the Eiffel Tower. Later, she would become the concertmistress with L' Orchestre National de France.

The origins of *When Paris Was Her Lover* were in Paris itself. I was visiting a dear friend, Anne Houssay. She showed me her workplace at the Musée de la Musique, where she studied and restored the most valuable stringed instruments on this planet. At the end of this monumental visit, she handed me a pamphlet and told me she thought I might be interested in the topic. Later that day, when I was back on the plane, I pulled it out and began to read the words. I was instantly riveted, moved, and inspired. I knew then that upon my return to my writing desk, a book would emerge.

Thank you profoundly, Anne, for introducing me to *Musique et Spoliations: Recherche de Provenance des Instruments et Documents Musicaux* (Looted Music: Tracing Looted Instruments and Musical Material).

Another beautiful human being and dear friend, Chloé Laroche, introduced me to Romanian adoptions. One year I visited her near Grenoble, France, and I was honored to meet her gorgeous new daughter, Julia, whom she and her then husband had adopted from Romania. This child, a product of the brutal era of the Ceausescu dictatorship, arrived with multiple challenges, yet each of these Chloe met with her consistent love and care. Over all the years that Julia has grown and matured, Chloé has shown me how love can truly transform a human being. Thank you, dear Chloé.

A huge thank-you goes to my friend Brune D'Esna, who gave me permission to use one of her photos for the cover of my book, a timeless glimpse of Paris, one that` captures the true essence of this magical city of her origins.

Another huge thank-you goes to the amazing book cover artist, Clare Colins. She put together a brilliant piece of art that blends this timeless beauty of Paris with the red earth of Australia and the magnificence of the violin…underneath there is the horror of war, yet her art reminds us of the transcendence from the pathos of the human existence to that of the sublime, survival in its quintessential realm.

Thank you, Karen Windhorn, director of the Early Childhood Program at the Rochester School for the Deaf, for providing me with your wisdom and your inspiring facts regarding language development in the young Deaf child.

Thank you to my editors for the behind-the-scenes work that transforms a banal piece of writing into that which stands out, alone, ready to be recognized: Elizabeth DeNoma and Beth Partin.

Thank you to Kathy Campbell of Gorham Printing for your expertise and for the beautiful work you did on the cover and book design. Thank you to everyone else at Gorham Printing for turning my MS Word document into the book you are holding in your hands.

There were times during the writing of this book when we forgot how to embrace others. COVID avoidance disorder, I called it, fear of touching another. I drew the line, though, with my precious mother. At ninety-two, she, the Holocaust survivor, reminds me constantly of how survival and love link together. I adore, treasure, respect, admire, and mostly love love love you, my precious mama.

And lastly, is it too presumptuous to show gratitude to oneself? The hurdles were huge: fibromyalgia, which often thrashes me about with unruly thorns coupled with COVID anxiety and frequent exhaustion. One night, I had a dream of opening a publishing house for not just my books, but others'. In the metaphor of dreams are real thoughts. I know there are as many stories out there that need to be in print as there are drops of rain that do not fall in a drought. On the first day of February, the beginning of the water tiger year, my year, I waited in line at the county clerk's office. Amid happy couples getting their marriage license, I walked out, holding in my hand a thin piece of paper that announced that Emerald House Publishing was born.

What you now hold in your hands…or on your phone…is a product of dreams, not just the one I had that night, but dreams of doing something that challenged me so immensely that I at times cried myself to sleep at night with exhaustion…only to wake up the next morning buoyed by my exuberant self that knew it was creating something significantly immense.

Pride can be a very moving thing.

Please join me in celebrating and honoring dreams: mine, yours, our planet's…

HEIDI HARRISON, author of *The Four Seasons* (Sapphire Books Publishing), has always loved writing. At an early age, she realized that words allowed for the exodus of her soul, a rhapsody, a sense of grace enveloping her. Writing has been her boulder, her stories the healing balm in a world that sometimes cries out for this. She was born and raised in the San Francisco Bay Area. She holds a Master of Science degree in counseling psychology and a dual degree in child development and French, and she spent almost thirty years as a psychotherapist and a teacher of young children. She is also a classically trained violinist. She has traveled extensively between the hemispheres and has lived and studied in Paris and in Grenoble, France. She has written several novels and children's books, countless stories (fiction and creative nonfiction), and a full-length memoir. In each of these works, she is inspired by imagination itself, by real stories of people's lives, by love, by music, by the stunning majesty of nature, by the beauty and power of words, relationships, the diversity of cultures, and the resilience of the human heart. We live in a complicated and often challenging world, and yet, as a writer, an observer, and a teacher, she is, every day, inspired by the grace and by the infinite beauty that we, as humans, embody. Our dazzling earth is of an infinite nature; humbly, she lets words only begin to describe it.

Her stories have been published in *The Sun* magazine and *Still Point Arts Quarterly* magazine.

When Paris Was Her Lover is her second published novel. It won an honorable mention in the 2019 Landmark Prize for Fiction with Homebound Publications.

Writer's website: www.heidimharrison.com

Facebook: https://www.facebook.com/HeidiEmeraldHarrison.Author/

Emerald House Publishing website: www.emeraldhpublishing.com